VOLUME I
SERENITY

BI-CURIOUS VOLUME 1:

SERENITY

NATALIE WEBER

URBAN BOOKS
www.urbanbooks.net

Urban Books, LLC
78 East Industry Court
Deer Park, NY 11729

ISBN 13: 978-1-60162-435-2
ISBN 10: 1-60162-435-2

First Printing February 2011
Printed in the United States of America

10 9 8 7 6 5 4 3 2 1

Distributed by Kensington Publishing Corp.
Submit Wholesale Orders to:
Kensington Publishing Corp.
C/O Penguin Group (USA) Inc.
Attention: Order Processing
405 Murray Hill Parkway
East Rutherford, NJ 07073-2316
Phone: 1-800-526-0275
Fax: 1-800-227-9604

Prologue

Serenity's tears flowed down her cheeks, and she couldn't stop her legs from quivering as she was in clear view of the camcorder. She sat in a wooden chair positioned perfectly centered with the camera's lens. Her disheveled hair covered the right side of her face making this beautiful young woman look like a tortured soul in distress. She couldn't believe the words that were about to come out of her mouth, but it was something that she had to do. She looked at the solid red light on top of the camera, indicating that it was recording, and took a couple of deep breaths before she began to speak. Trembling, she wiped the blood dripping from her nose before she spoke to the camera.

"I have been through so much this last year, and I am at the end of my rope. I saw the love of my life die . . . because of me," Serenity cried. "I killed Rock!" She began to weep harder.

Serenity tried to regain her composure. She gripped her head tightly and began to hyperventilate as she thought about what was about to come out of her mouth. She looked over at the stand to the right of her and picked up the small syringe filled with a lethal substance. Snot and tears continued to flow as she shook her head, trying to convince herself not to go through with the plan. Then her trembling fingers picked up the syringe and placed it to her arm as she stared into the camera. Serenity began to wonder how she had put herself in the position she was currently in. Holding the needle to her arm, she whispered to the camera one last time.

"I don't want to live anymore."

Students gathered around in front of the big JumboTron that sat in the middle of the college campus in complete shock and stunned silence. They were witnessing their fellow classmate confessing to a murder in front of the whole campus. It was noon, the usual time when many of the students gathered for lunch at the central campus. All of the students were totally devastated as they watched. Most of them thought it was a prank, but it was far more serious than they could ever imagine. Just before Serenity could push the poison filled the needle into her arm, the screen went blank, leaving everyone speechless.

Chapter One

One year earlier

"Oh, right there, ma," the girl said, grinding her hips into Carla's face. Carla's eyes were closed, and her hands were gripping her lover's plump buttocks as she licked her sweet flower. The girl's legs were straight up in the air and spread wide apart. Serenity couldn't help but watch through the crack of the door that gave her a wonderful voyeuristic view.

She entered the house about ten minutes earlier and heard moaning coming from the back room. It was her older sister, Carla, who was so busy serving her lover that she didn't hear Serenity enter. Serenity was not a lesbian, but there was something inside of her urging her to see how they got down. She had been watching her sister and her lover since she walked in and couldn't pull herself away from peeking behind the bedroom door. She watched Carla grinding her midsection into the bed while she gave her lover oral pleasure. Serenity didn't want to admit it, but it was a beautiful sight—to see two women show their sexual desire for each other.

The girl and Carla switched positions. Now Carla was on her back with a face full of plump, succulent breasts and erect nipples. The girl rode Carla's pussy as if it was a man's hard pipe—with precision and seductive rhythm. Serenity couldn't help notice the beautiful, colored tattooed butterfly on the girl's ass. It was flawless, and her movement formed a wave motion. Carla held both of her lover's breasts together and licked on her nipples. As her tongue caressed the nipples, her lover moved closer to her climax.

Serenity's love box began to pulsate, noticing how well they knew how to please each other in the most intimate of ways. *Men have the tendency of being overly aggressive and sometimes move too fast. But women have the preciseness of a surgeon and a connection on an emotional level most men could care less about*, she thought. She was brought back to reality by the loud moans from the lovers as they reached their climax. It made Serenity hot and curious to find out—if her love box could withstand the pressure. By now her clit was thumping wildly. She quickly turned her head and silently walked away from the door.

What the fuck! I'm not gay, she thought. She tried to erase the images out of her head. She walked to the front door, opened it, and slammed it back closed to let her sister know she was in the house. Then she walked into the living room, plopped down on the sofa, and turned on the TV. About fifteen minutes later, Carla walked in wearing her robe.

"Hey, sis," she said as she walked to the kitchen.

"What's up, Carla?" Serenity asked as she browsed her DVR list.

Carla returned to the living room with a bottle of water and sat down on the sofa across from Serenity.

"My baby sister is all grown-up now. How does it feel to be finished with school?"

"It feels good, I guess," Serenity said, still thinking about Carla's "friend" who waited for her in the back.

Serenity had gotten used to seeing a lot of girls come in and out of her sister's life. Carla is what you called a "stud." A "stud" in the lesbian world was the dominant person in a girl-on-girl relationship and usually dressed masculine. She had short hair, hazel eyes, a light complexion, and she wore two diamond earrings on her right ear. She dressed in designer jeans, a T-shirt, and a pair of the latest kicks out. Serenity wondered why Carla dressed like a guy when she was so stunning whenever she dressed as a female.

Carla was financially responsible for Serenity. Carla was a "hustler." She moved cocaine throughout the Midwest. She had the purest cocaine around, which came from her D.C. connect. Serenity knew exactly what her sister did to get money, but she never said a word about it. She figured the less she knew, the better.

"Momma would be so proud of you," Carla said, moving next to Serenity and putting her arm around her.

Serenity smiled, thinking about how her big sister

had been her sole provider and protector since their mother died of cancer years earlier. Their father was sent to the state penitentiary for a life sentence on a murder charge just before she turned two years old. Carla had always looked out for her baby sister. She had always liked girls, but she didn't come out of the closet until their mother died. That's when she finally cut her hair off and lived the lifestyle she wanted to. She had swagger and the looks that drew every lesbian after her within the city of Chicago, and, at times, beyond the city limits.

Although Carla and Serenity were on opposite ends of the spectrum, their bond was something no one could ever break.

"Yeah, she would be proud. And she would be really proud of you. You know that, right?" Serenity asked. She looked at her sister and smiled.

"Yeah, I know, but you are the first to go to college. The few classes I took don't count. You're getting that paper, that degree. Ain't no way you gonna be in these streets like me. Let's be for real. You'll be an adult soon. You know what I do to get this cash. So let's not avoid the fucking pink elephant in the room. What's on your mind?" Carla questioned, seriously.

"Well, you sure you wanna bring this up now?" Serenity thoughtfully reminded her about her intimate friend back in the room.

"What? You talking about that bitch back in the room?" Carla said harshly.

"Damn, why you always gotta get all hype?" Serenity asked, cautioning her sister about her temper.

"Okay, I didn't mean to get loud, but I am trying to let you know that you can do a whole lot of things that I never could do. You hear me, this is some real talk."

"I know. Well, I was thinking of getting a job while I'm at school to help you out," Serenity spoke in a soft voice.

"No, no, no!" Carla said with annoyance, and then took a deep breath. "Look, I don't mean it like that. Don't worry, I got you. Whichever school you pick, it's covered," Carla promised, giggling.

"What's so funny?" Serenity asked, trying to hold on to a straight face.

"Nah, it's just that whatever school you pick—" Carla said, then burst into a high-pitched laugh at the thought of the position she would soon be in. "Serenity, can you imagine the looks that I'll receive when I pay the school."

"Yeah, I can only picture those faces. Hey, come to think about it, that's gonna be good for me too. I can probably get a little prestige at school with money behind me," Serenity said in her snottiest of attitudes, and they both busted out into laughter.

"Yeah, I hear you, sis. Just don't get a bigger head, but seriously, have you gotten any letters back from those colleges you applied to?" Carla asked.

"Yeah, I got a few of them back. Howard University, Central State, VSU, and NYU accepted me, but . . . I think . . . I'm going to go to the smaller private school out in D.C. I think you know which one . . ." Serenity answered bowing her head.

"Oh, really . . . So I guess my feelings *are* right. You going to follow that nigga of yours, ain't ya?" she asked referring to Serenity's boyfriend who already attended the small private college.

"Maybe," Serenity said with a grin, walking to the bathroom to take a shower. Her sister followed her. "I'm going out with Rock tonight. I probably won't be back 'til late, okay?" Serenity said, leaning against the opened door. "We can talk more about it later."

"Yeah, a'ight, that's cool. I got company anyway. So, it's whatever floats your boat. I'm 'bout to chef something up for dinner. I done worked up an appetite," Carla said and rubbed on her stomach, then walked away from Serenity toward the kitchen.

Carla hated the fact that Serenity was with Rock. She heard about him doing some deals with her connect in D.C., and now he's running a high-end weed service. He was fucking some dyke chick before he started to go to school there. Ever since Carla found that out, she couldn't stand him. She wanted him hurt, so she got some of her people to beat him up every time he came around Serenity. Whether he came to see her at her school, at the mall, in the park—wherever he went and Serenity was around, he was going to catch a beat down. Carla just wanted him to leave her sister alone. She thought it would work, but she didn't count on him not giving up. After five weeks of beatings, Carla gave up on trying to separate them.

Carla knew that Serenity and Rock had been sneaking around for a little more than a year, but hadn't realized how strong their feelings were for each other until he refused to stop seeing Serenity. She would hear her sister cry after every beating Rock received. Serenity pleaded with Carla to leave him alone. Carla didn't want him to come between the only family she had. Finally, she called the "on-sight beatings" off and let them be. And even after all that, to this day, she and Rock still hadn't spoken more than a few words to each other.

Carla tried to clue Serenity in on how Rock was really getting down, but her sister refused to listen.

Now that she learned Serenity was going to the same college as Rock, she was not happy. Carla wanted to know even more about how much paper he had, his drug-hustling status, and how hot and heavy he was with any other females.

Serenity stepped into her room wrapped in a white towel and sat at her vanity mirror. She looked into her sea-green eyes and said to herself, "Why don't you just ask your sister about it?" She quickly stood and went to her closet to pick out her outfit for the night. *It needs to be something new*, she thought. Before she opened her closet door, she caught a glimpse of herself in the full-length mirror. As she stood there, she dropped her towel and stared at her naked body. *Can I really be gay? Do I really want to find out what another woman's touch is like? How can I find out without Rock being involved?* The thoughts tumbled in her mind.

Her striking eyes complemented her light complexion. Slowly, she placed her hands on her breasts and admired their firmness. Her nipples began to stiffen. She lightly circled her fingertips around them, then slowly moved one of her hands against her flat stomach and closed her eyes as she pretended another woman was exploring her body. Soon, her fingers wandered south to her clit. Now she opened her eyes and watched herself stroke her clit with the lightest touch of her fingertip. She continued to tease herself as she pinched her nipples. Before long, she began to feel her juices trickling down between her legs. Caught in the moment, she allowed her fingertip to gently rub against her wet opening; then she returned to toy with her clit.

Serenity's mind was filled with images of beautiful, naked women with their hands all over her—touching her, wanting her, and tantalizing her with their tongues. *Why is it so hard for my man to do it?* she wondered. She snapped out of her spontaneous foreplay, grabbed her towel, wrapped it around her now lustful, aching body, and opened her closet door. She needed to suppress this conflict within herself.

Serenity searched her closet for the shopping bags her sister gave her the other day. She found the Gucci bag. It had a drop-dead, short, black skirt that would make anyone look like a deer in headlights. There was also a gorgeous, popping blue-colored blouse to go with it—not to mention the neckline that plunged damn near to her belly button. She would have to wear her four-inch black stiletto heels from Ferragamo. She immediately rushed back to the bathroom to shower again.

Serenity quickly began her routine: she would put on her favorite CD for that week, rub her Shea Butter lotion on her body, then do her hair, get dressed, apply makeup, and splash on Chanel No. 5 to finish—on those *very* special spots. She believed tonight would be an unforgettable night.

Serenity walked into the kitchen to get her sister's approval of her outfit. "Hey, what you think?"

"Serenity, what you tryin' to do? You know exactly what he's going to want dressed like that, girl," Carla blurted out.

"What you trying to say?" Serenity asked with a hint of attitude.

"Nah, it's not even like that! I mean, you look like the shit, girl! Ain't nobody fucking with you on your looks. Damn, I know how to pick an outfit! I should of kept that for one of *my* girls," Carla replied finishing up dinner.

"What you talking 'bout sis? Surprised that I actually listened to you on how to get everyone, including the same sex, to look when I step into a room?" Serenity laughed. Her cell phone vibrated in her hand; it was her boyfriend, Rock.

He had promised her he would take her out to a dinner and a nightclub to celebrate her graduation. His summer break had already begun from school, so he was at home for the past couple of weeks, spending every day with her.

Serenity put up her finger to signal to her sister to be quiet. Her face lit up instantly once she answered the phone.

"Hey, ma," Rock said before she could even say a word.

"Hey, baby. I missed you," she said walking toward the window. She looked out the window of the two-story house and saw his black Porsche Cayenne SUV with those twenty-two's sparkling like diamonds parked in front of her house.

"I missed you too, girl. Now come on out and don't keep me waiting. I want to see your sexy ass," Rock said just before he flipped his phone down.

Serenity hurried into the bathroom and checked her hair and makeup. Just as quickly as she did that, she was already heading for the door. "Be back later to-night, sis! Enjoy your dinner. It looks good," she said as she sprinted past Carla and closed the door. Serenity couldn't wait to start her celebration with her man.

Rock put his phone away. He took his last pull of the blunt and dumped it in the ashtray. He couldn't wait for Serenity to start college. He knew all the key players there and knew if his plans went right, his wildest fantasies would be fulfilled.

Serenity opened the door to Rock's SUV and was greeted with a smile and the strong scent of weed. By the looks of his red eyes, she could tell Rock just finished smoking a blunt. His thick eyebrows, chocolate-toned skin, and juicy lips looked better than ever to her.

Rock had been her man ever since freshman year of high school. He was in love with her. He was two years her senior and was the one who took her virginity. She had no other experiences with any other man. He explored her body and taught her everything she knew about sex and her sensuality.

"Hey, ma," he said as he leaned over to kiss her.

Serenity smiled back and kissed him, then got comfortable in his butter-soft leather seat. "Hey, baby . . . Where we going tonight?" she asked, moving her hand up her leg enticingly until she reached her panties.

"Wow, baby girl, my dick is hard," Rock said trying to adjust his now-erect penis in his pants. "We might have to x that dinner and shit and go directly to the hotel, ya hear?" Rock quickly turned into traffic.

"Oh, stop it. You promised to celebrate; you just didn't say which was first," Serenity said, grinning from ear-to-ear. She knew her body was already tuned up for a hot escape.

"Okay, you wanna go to that spot?" Rock quickly seized the moment.

"No, I really want you to make me cum. You know how," Serenity started to nibble at his ear while trying to unbuckle his belt.

"Now you know that shit ain't happening," Rock said, confidently brushing her hand away.

"Oh, come on, baby. You done it before. Why can't you do it to me?" Serenity asked in disappointment.

"Come on, I don't wanna wreck my plans 'cause we got into an argument. Tonight we're celebrating. I'm going to make it official," Rock said slyly flashing a grin. "You just relax, put your head back, baby, let me show you a good time," he said, and turned to face her.

Serenity smiled, knowing he had something up his sleeve. He always did. That was one of the things that attracted her to him. Ever since they first met, she remembered his swagger, impeccable appearance, and his popularity with all the girls. She fell for him at her very first glance—she would never let him know it though—of his smooth, milk chocolate skin bulging through his T-shirt, his dreamy brown eyes, and the smell of his cologne when he passed her in the hallway of school. Serenity looked at his handsome profile as he drove, and she wanted to devour him right then and there. Instead, she reached for his hand and placed it on her thigh. She loved that feeling—his touch.

Rock knew that Serenity had no idea he planned an evening of elegance and pure seduction. He had one question only, and on this night, he hoped Serenity would give him the answer he had been waiting for because he was ready. He turned onto a gravel road that led to a pier.

Serenity looked out her passenger-side window and saw a private yacht with the name *Everlasting* painted on its side. She couldn't believe her eyes. Rock had never taken her anywhere as upscale as this. *What's he really celebrating? Could this be it? He and I forever?*

Rock drove onto the pier and stopped. The doors were opened by two men. Serenity, smiled at them.

"Good evening, sir," Rock was greeted by one of the crew members.

"Yes, beautiful evening and hopefully a wonderful night," Rock said, watching Serenity climb out of the truck.

"Right this way, sir. Everything is on schedule. Kimberly is waiting for you at the boarding entrance," one crew member said.

"Thanks," Rock replied. He handed the guy a crisp fifty-dollar bill and walked toward Serenity.

"Rock, what's going on? When you said we were celebrating you never mentioned *this*," Serenity said, nervous with excitement, walking toward the boarding entrance.

"Baby, I told you, relax and enjoy. It's your night. Can we go eat and have a few drinks?" he said, and grabbed Serenity's hand.

"Hello, sir, welcome to the *Everlasting*. Please come aboard," Kimberly said, smiling and leading the young couple to the bow of the yacht.

Serenity saw a table covered in the prettiest soft green linen, set with lit candles, a bouquet of white roses as the centerpiece, and sparkling silverware. Champagne was sitting in a bucket of ice next to the table.

They sat next to each other, and Kimberly poured

each of them a glass of Dom Perignon Rose champagne in the twin emerald-green Marsala champagne flutes and then left.

Serenity looked at Rock with wonder and amazement. "Rock, is everything all right?"

"Of course, what's up? You don't like this?" he asked, with his hand motioning their surroundings.

"No, I love it. I'm just surprised. I can't believe you would do all this when I only just graduated high school. I can't even legally drink yet. Aren't these people gonna get in trouble?" Serenity asked, concerned.

"No one is gonna get in trouble 'cause you had a little champagne, baby. Besides, I got this for a few hours," Rock said, and handed Serenity her glass. "Now, I would like to toast you, my baby. You deserve everything you desire, and I will be the man to provide it. This is just a start." Rock raised his glass to hers and tapped it gently.

Serenity sipped her champagne, then gently kissed him on the lips. "Thank you."

Kimberly returned with a silver tray in her hands and placed a small Greek salad dotted with Feta cheese in front of each of them.

"Enjoy your first of six courses," Kimberly smiled.

"Thanks," Serenity and Rock chimed in unison.

The two lovers sat there engrossed in good conversation, delicious food, and feeling a nice buzz off the two bottles of Dom Perignon they shared throughout dinner.

Rock looked at his woman and licked his lips while admiring her beauty. He had been planning on introducing her to the idea of a ménage à trois that night, and he was waiting for the perfect time to present his proposal. He wanted to have a threesome with his girl, but when he mentioned it before, she brushed it off as a joke and paid it no mind. But, he wasn't joking. He wanted to see another female lick Serenity's pinkness while he watched.

"You know I love you, right?" Rock asked and slowly sipped his drink. He stared at Serenity.

"Yeah, I know, baby. You my sweetheart, the love of my life," she said, reaching for his hand.

"I've been thinking, ya know. I want to take our relationship to the next level," Rock said, then took another sip from his glass.

"What are you getting at, Rock? What's the next level?" Serenity asked, eager to find out what Rock was talking about.

"Before I ask you this, I want you to promise me that you will keep an open mind and at least hear me out before you interrupt me," he said displaying his alluring smile.

"Rock, I already know yo ass . . . I am *not* letting a female eat my pussy. You got me twisted! We have gone over this shit a thousand fuckin' times. I knew what you were going to say when you gave me the same dumbass, tell-all smile you always give me before you ask me that shit," Serenity snapped and stood up from the table, furious that he would actually go this far to have a threesome.

"Am I that obvious?" Rock replied, standing. He gave

her a look of defeat, knowing that he had lost the battle before it even started.

"Yes, you are! I can't believe you did all this to ask me that. What did you think? I would say yes 'cause of this luxury, or was it the fuckin' champagne? Here I am thinking the next level was making our fuckin' relationship stronger, and the only reason you did all this was because you want some next bitch to fuck me? Fuck you, Rock. That shit ain't happening. I'm ready to leave. You sure know how to fuck up someone's night. Just get me the fuck outta here," Serenity shot back and folded her arms.

Every time Rock asked her about this new sexual experience, she would quickly turn him down, but secretly, she wondered how it would feel to let another female lick her hot spot—Rock could never know the truth.

Serenity remembered overhearing her sister a while back. She was in a deep discussion with some of her male friends. She stated no one knows how to satisfy a woman better than a woman. She also said that women have a way of soothing another woman's clit that couldn't be matched by any man. The ego of a man always got in the way. In some strange way, a man got jealous of his own tongue and never wanted his oral sex to out beat his own penis. She said a man would never fully commit to eating a woman's pussy, letting foolish pride get in the way.

The statement always had her thinking about how it

would feel for another woman to sooth her desire. The way Carla put it, it made so much sense to her.

Serenity stood in front of Rock with what felt like steam coming out of her ears.

Rock reached for her hands and gently placed them on top of his shoulders. He lightly positioned his fingers on her hips and whispered, "I'm sorry. I really did all this for you. That's it, nothing else. I just thought since the night was going so well I would sneak that request in. I didn't want you to get this upset about it. Damn. And another thing, that threesome shit is not on top of my list. But, if you ready to 'fuckin' go, as you put it, then let me alert the captain to turn this motherfucka around 'cause my girl got highly upset with me 'cause I asked her to have a threesome, okay?" he said with the slightest hint of annoyance. He surely didn't want her to think that she was right.

"Oh my God, Rock! You wouldn't dare, would you?"

"Oh, yes, I would. Watch me." Rock immediately turned around to pretend he was heading toward the crew members' headquarters. He was hoping Serenity would reach out to stop him, or else he would be the fool.

"Rock, stop . . . I'm sorry. I didn't mean to react like that. I just thought you meant something else. Let's just go back to our seats and enjoy the rest of this night. I don't wanna fight," she said, putting her arms around him.

Rock kissed her with such passion, she forgot all about the theatrics. She knew how the night would end—in hot, zealous sex. She was willing to let everything go. She wanted him so bad that she didn't care how stupid he was acting—even if he didn't think so.

"This my pussy, right?" Rock asked, gently separating Serenity's plump butt cheeks and stroking her from behind.

"Yes. It's yours, daddy," Serenity crooned, rubbing her own clit and slowly thrusting her backside at him.

They were in perfect rhythm on the park bench. It was their secret spot. It was in a low-key park on the east side of Chicago. They couldn't wait to get back to Rock's crib. They wanted each other so badly.

Rock let his thumb slip over Serenity's other hole, rubbing it softly, while stuffing her wet pussy with his hard dick.

"Ooh, fuck me, baby," Serenity hummed as she felt her butthole being massaged. She loved the way it made her feel. A chill went up her body, and she felt an orgasm approaching. "Keep hitting it, baby . . . Get that spot, daddy . . ." she demanded as she gripped the bench and threw her backside even harder at him.

"Aw, shit," Rock whispered, while tightening his grip on Serenity's ass. His strokes became faster, and he felt the lovely sensation of his nut nearing him. He couldn't stop himself from exploding.

Serenity knew that tone oh too well. She knew she only had a few seconds to try to catch hers before he shot off.

"Here it comes, ba—" Rock exclaimed as he climaxed.

"Don't cum yet, baby . . . please, baby, not yet!" Serenity screamed, trying her best to jiggle her ass to keep him hard for just a little longer, but it was too late. His strokes had changed, and his hard pipe was now just a limp noodle inside of her. "Damn, Rock, I told you to hold on," Serenity said with displeasure. She came to grips with the fact that she wouldn't be totally satisfied that night—twice.

"I'm sorry, baby girl. It was feeling too good. I couldn't hold it in," Rock said quickly sliding out of her and pulling up his pants.

Serenity smacked her lips and pulled down her skirt. She folded her arms across her chest and showed her disappointment. She hated when he left her hanging. It was becoming more frequent lately. *I only get some from him once every blue moon since he's been in college, and he pulls this shit?* she thought sitting on the bench, watching Rock buckle his belt.

He was smiling confidently. He looked like he had just scored the winning touchdown for his team.

Serenity was upset with him. *Now what? We go back to his crib to sleep? This motherfucker got some nerve. Whatever happened to wanting me to cum too?*

Rock was against exploring down below with his tongue because of his past relationships. When he did finally come around to doing it, he found out they were cheating every time. He was completely turned off. He never planned on doing it again. He had left Serenity without an orgasm plenty of times before, but it was evident she was growing tired of it. He thought maybe he should just give in to her. After all, he knew who she was fucking.

Nevertheless, Serenity loved Rock and his little imperfection wasn't a big enough cause for her to cheat on him. This was just one of many hot summer love episodes with him. But her world would be shaken up as soon as she stepped foot on campus.

It was the place both their lives changed forever.

Chapter Two

The summer passed, and Serenity finally was a freshman in college. She and Carla had driven all the way to D.C. from their hometown, Chicago. It took all day and almost all night to make it to the college.

Carla wanted to make sure Serenity got there safe and settled in correctly. She planned on bringing some weight back from her cocaine connect, which was just an added bonus. And she wanted to check out the campus and see if she might bump into this chick she heard about.

Serenity didn't know, but Carla did some fact checking into her baby sister's new surroundings and what she may get into. She heard about the wild parties and the big players. She really wanted to see if this female she heard of was around. The word was that this female was a stud like her. Someone who had a yearning to turn out many straight freshmen just for fun. They would all eventually turn into drug-addicted sex slaves for her benefit and enjoyment.

Carla wanted to make sure this female knew that her sister was not to be fucked with. She would never forgive herself if anything happened to Serenity.

They pulled up to the school with a look of disappointment on their faces. The school was located in the heart of a ghetto. It was obvious to them both that getting an off-campus apartment was out of the question.

Serenity was thinking that a car would be necessary. She immediately made her sister aware of what she wanted.

After the initial shock of where they were wore off, Serenity stepped out of the car. She looked around to see many new students off-loading their things out of their cars. A check-in table stood nearby, so she walked over to retrieve her assigned dorm room location.

As she got in line, her attention was caught by this attractive guy standing not too far from the table. He had an olive complexion and gorgeous face. He should have been a woman. His designer clothes and colorful taste in sneakers proved that he had great taste. By all the females surrounding him, Serenity knew he was one of the elite.

"Excuse me, what's your last name? You're not the only one here," the young lady said with an attitude.

Serenity was snapped away from her eye candy. She looked at the female and said, "Sorry, um . . . White, Serenity White."

"Thank you. Here are your keys, room location, and

welcome package. Please read everything. If you got any questions or need your schedule changed, please go to the Web site address on the front of your welcome package. Got it?"

"Yeah, thanks." Serenity snatched her package out of the girl's hand and quickly returned to the car.

"What happened? Just a minute ago you were excited. Now what?" Carla asked, seeing the pissed-off look on Serenity's face.

"Damn, I just got here and bitches wanna start," Serenity murmured.

"Oh, come on, it can't be all that bad. Calm down. Who the fuck cares 'bout them bitches anyway? Remember they're there to help you," Carla reminded her.

"It's just that I was . . . okay, I admit it. I wasn't paying attention. Damn, you always know when it's my fault," Serenity said, playfully pushing her sister.

"Let's get this shit up to your room so I can go handle some business and go home. Finally, I can live alone," Carla laughed.

"What you mean?" Serenity searched for the truth.

"Just kidding. Damn, it ain't like you going to be at home any time soon," Carla replied.

"Well, you better not do nothing to my room or have any one of your trick-ass females up in there. Trust me, I *will* be home come every holiday and vacation. You heard, now get my shit upstairs." Serenity laughed at her own words.

They began the task of moving her things into her new living space.

Finished, both of them finally sat on the bed, exhausted from bringing all the boxes up to the dorm room. Serenity had on a tight-fitting jogging suit, while her sister wore baggy pants and a white T-shirt. They lay on the bed, too tired to even speak from all the lugging up and down, back and forth.

"Well, this is it," Carla said, looking up at the ceiling while still breathing heavily. She wiped the sweat from her brow and sat up.

"Yeah, I'm finally in college," Serenity answered, sitting up and looking around.

Carla leaned back on her elbows and looked around the tiny room, examining it. They noticed that the twin bed in the opposite corner was already made up. A rainbow designed comforter was neatly folded at the foot of the bed, signaling that Serenity's roommate had already moved in.

"I hope I don't have an annoying-ass roommate," Serenity said in an exasperated tone.

"You never know," Carla answered.

On cue, the door opened and a tall, slender girl with dark, ebony skin came through the door. She wore tight, skinny jeans and a fresh pair of Pastry sneakers were on her small feet. Her Chinese-cut bangs hid her forehead and drew more attention to her green eyes—obviously contact lenses.

Carla and the girl's eyes locked, and both of them grew grins on their faces. It was an instant attraction.

"Hello, there," the girl said while placing the tip of her manicured nail between her two front teeth.

"What up, ma," Carla said rising up with a male's swagger.

"I'm Raya," the girl said, holding out her hand.

"I'm Carla," she said, doing her best LL Cool J impression. She took Raya's hand and shook it gently with a glimpse of her perfect smile.

Serenity just sat and watched as she instantly became the third wheel. There was an awkward silence in the room as Carla and Raya just stared into each other's eyes, neither of them letting go of their trance. Serenity grew tired of watching the two of them look at each other in awe, smiling like teenagers. She quickly decided to break up the lost-in-translation moment between them.

"Uh-hum," Serenity cleared her throat and stood up, snapping both women out of their adolescent trance.

"Oh, yeah, this is my sister, Serenity. Your roommate," Carla said looking over at her sister.

"Too bad, I thought *you* were my new roommate," Raya said, never taking her eyes off Carla. She leaned in closer to Carla and whispered just loud enough, "We could of had so much fun."

"Hello," Serenity said, extending her hand.

Raya smiled and stepped past Carla so she could shake Serenity's hand. "Hey, girl, I'm Raya, and this is my side of the room," she said walking over to her bed to sit down with her legs partially open. "I'm on the squad too."

"Yeah, I can see that."

"Ain't you funny . . ." she said, smiling. "Yup, this going to be fun."

Carla's eyes shot down to Raya's crotch. Her camel toe was on full display through her tight jeans.

Carla involuntarily licked her lips, imaging how she could use her gifted tongue to play with Raya's clit and take her to new heights.

"Yeah, uh-huh . . . ," Serenity turned to her sister and mouthed, "this is whack." She went back to unpacking. There was something about Raya that she didn't like, so she kept it short and sweet.

On the other hand, there was something about Raya that Carla couldn't get enough of. Carla only wished that she could stick around and have fun with Raya, but she was there for one purpose only and that was making sure her sister got moved in comfortably.

"Well, I'm about to go to the registration office to get my schedule. I forgot to pick it up when I checked in. I'll leave you two to talk," Serenity lied.

They didn't even respond to her comment as they kept eye contact with each other—both of them thinking the exact same thing.

As soon as Serenity exited, the two women were drawn to each other like magnets.

Carla began to lick Raya's neck.

Raya moaned passionately and rubbed Carla's back.

They both knew that they didn't have a lot of time. They just wanted to get their nut off.

It didn't take long for Raya to strip off her jeans and

lay flat on her back. With her legs wide open, Carla lowered her head and began to move her tongue like an untamed beast. She was driving Raya wild. Raya had only felt this way once before. And it had been a long time since then.

The way Carla flicked at her love button was accurate and on point. She hit the spot with every lick, all the while two fingers plunged into Raya's wetness ever so deep, just enough for Raya to feel it.

Raya was going totally insane as she squirmed like a fish fresh out of the water. "Ooh, shit!" she yelled, pushing Carla's face deeper into her pink folds.

Carla had no problem getting to the treasure since she was hairless down under. A small puddle of juice began to form right under Raya's butt, and it was turning her on. Carla was getting moist just by the moans alone coming from Raya's lips. At this point, it was all about getting off. She felt Raya's body begin to tremble, knowing an orgasm was approaching. Carla quickly stopped and stood up.

Raya didn't stop squirming. She began to play with herself.

Carla dropped her pants, exposing her Calvin Klein boxers. She quickly removed her boxers and climbed on top of Raya; then she spread her pussy lips, exposing her clit that stuck out like a miniature penis. Gently, she placed it directly on top of Raya's clit.

They both began to grind on each other, climbing toward an orgasm. The sounds of their bodies slamming against each other filled the air, and the grinding movement became faster and harder for the both of them as they peaked and climaxed together.

Then Carla collapsed on top of Raya. Both of them smiled, completely satisfied with each other.

"What's your name again?" Carla said, causing both of them to burst out into laughter.

"That was fun. Maybe we can do it again when you come to visit," Raya said, starting to get dressed. She didn't want Serenity to think she was free like that with everyone she first met.

Carla looked at Raya and said, "Maybe, ma. But let's keep it real with each other. This was only a nut."

"For sure," Raya said with a slight disappointment in her tone. She then walked over to her desk, wrote her number on a Post-it, and handed it to Carla. "Here's my number just in case you change your mind." Then she walked out of the room and left Carla to wait for Serenity's return.

Serenity returned a short while later. "Hey, what happened to my roommate?"

"Ahh, she said she had to go check on something. I don't know!" Carla said avoiding eye contact with her sister. She didn't want her to feel uneasy knowing that she just did her roommate after their first encounter.

"Oh, okay. Well, anyway, did you at least get her number? I know that look when I see it." Serenity began to laugh, putting her sister at ease.

"Oh, so you do, huh? All right, I gotta handle some

business. I better get goin'. You gonna be a'ight, li'l sis?" Carla asked.

"Yeah, I'm good money. I guess since you stayin' out in D.C. for a few days to handle your 'business,' I'll holla at you when I find a ride I want," Serenity said.

"Nah, I'ma handle that. One of my boys got a whip that's for sale. He just got it too. Now he don't want it. Niggas with money to burn, what a fuckin' life. I definitely gotta get some trees for the time I'm here. I'll holla at you tomorrow to give you the keys, a'ight?" Carla said, reaching to hug her sister before she headed for the door.

"A'ight, you can go now. Ready to live the college life . . . good-bye . . . see ya soon . . ." Serenity said, shooing her sister to the door.

"Damn, can I at least get a hug from my sis?" Carla said with a look of concern.

"Oh, yeah, of course." Serenity embraced her sister and whispered, "Love you, sis. I couldn't do this without you."

"All right, enough of this lovey-dovey shit. Just remember you don't know everything that's out here in this big world they call college. I'm only a holla away. Oh, yeah, I almost forgot, here's some cash, and use this debit card for your books and stuff. Don't just spend it on clothes and bullshit either. A'ight, holla!" Carla wiped her brow, put her fitted cap back on, and walked out the door.

When the door closed, Serenity turned around and

smiled. She was finally going to make her own decisions. She was tired of her sister telling her what to do, how to act, where to go, and who to be friends with. Now she could just relax and not feel like someone was watching her every move. She loved her sister, but sometimes she was too overprotective.

Serenity heard loud music coming from outside. She quickly walked to the window.

Outside a slick black Bentley was parked, blaring the music of Eminem. Two people stood close to the car talking. One guy was dressed in all-black with a black Kangol hat on. The other was the same guy she saw earlier behind the check-in table. She recognized his brightly colored sneakers.

She nodded and said quietly, "He's just eye candy; nothing more, nothing less." She had a man who loved her. She just wished he would bow down to her in more ways than one. Well, now that she lived on campus, she was positive that her sex life was going to get heated. Seeing Rock every day and doing him every time would definitely fulfill her appetite.

After the first week, Serenity was overwhelmed. Between finding her classes, time spent in those classes, and studying, Serenity discovered that her time was cut to a minimum with Rock. Between his football practices and her trying to figure out what sorority to join, Rock dropped to the last item on her list. Her idea of seeing him every day and getting some loving was rapidly disappearing.

* * *

Carla brought the keys to a BMW 320 Series the day she was leaving to return to Chicago. Serenity loved it. It was definitely her—sleek and stylish.

A month had passed by now and Serenity finally got a handle on her schedule. She loved college life. She felt free. During her high school years, it was so hard to always be under a watchful eye—Carla's. It wasn't easy to sneak away from her. She was continuously on the lookout for game. Her sister knew her next move before she even made it.

Serenity spent all her down time with Rock. She found out that he was pretty popular on campus, and rightfully so. He was one of the star players on the football team. It also helped that he was tall, handsome, and his swagger was on point. She was happy to be seen with him around campus. She loved that her popularity was increasing daily.

The haters, groupies, and just the straight-up hoes came out in force. She knew that it would happen eventually. Now that people knew who she was, a new rumor popped off every other week. Serenity never hesitated to let a female know what her place was.

In the time of adjusting to her new routines in life, she shook off her premonitions about Raya. She discovered, after the first week, they had a class together. Actually, they had a lot in common to her surprise. Well, excluding the lesbian thing she had going on. Yet, Serenity did wonder if she, herself, might not be a little that way too.

Almost every night, she heard her roommate with a

different woman. How could she not? After all, they shared the same room. The soft moans alone would make Serenity lust for the touch of a female between her legs. These thoughts began to surround her mind daily.

The campus was always packed as some students made their way to their classes while the others stood around in various groups talking and fraternizing. One day, Serenity and Raya were by themselves eating lunch at a table overlooking the parking lot and scoping out the scenery.

"It's hot as hell out here today," Raya complained, twisting her hair into a bun.

"You ain't said nothing I don't already know. Damn, maybe we should go back inside," Serenity said, nodding her head. She looked thoughtfully at Raya. *I didn't know you looked so good. Maybe I should be a little more outgoing. Who knows? Maybe you can show me a few sweet things.* She nodded her head again.

Out of nowhere a cluster of people began to gather in the parking lot. A metallic red Lamborghini with dark tinted windows demanded everyone's attention. The blinging chrome rims were rotating in what seemed to be slow motion as it entered the parking lot. Its glossy paint job was gleaming and flawless.

A small smile spread across Raya's face. Her eyes were glued to the car.

Serenity looked at her companion's facial expression

and noticed the sudden change. She had the look of a woman in pure lust for some man. But in her case, it would have to be a woman. She thought, *Who's the mystery woman behind the wheel of this quarter-million dollar car? And why in the world is everyone, including Raya, captivated, as if a celebrity just stepped into our midst?*

"Who's that?" Serenity nonchalantly asked.

The car parked, and the butterfly doors lifted up, showing only the bottom half of the driver. A crisp, white Air Force One sneaker graced the pavement, the driver's face still a mystery.

"That's Sadie Smith. *She* is the man on campus," Raya said. She quickly whipped out her mirror and fixed her hair, then applied some shiny lip gloss.

Serenity saw how much Raya stared in admiration at the newcomer. She finally saw what the hype was all about.

Sadie stepped out of the car effortlessly. Her loose denim shorts hung perfectly below her knees. She removed her designer shades and hung them onto her stark white T-shirt. Her hat was tilted slightly to the left on her head and the color matched her sneakers perfectly. Sadie was half Black and half Hispanic, giving her a Mediterranean appearance.

Serenity felt her face flush. She was embarrassed. She couldn't believe that she was looking at a *woman*. It was the very same person who caught her attention when she first arrived on campus with her sister. She had thought she was checking out a fine-ass man. *How could that happen? I know what a stud looks like*, she thought. She didn't realize that she too was staring now.

People began to flock to the car as if it were the main exhibit at a car show. Everyone out on campus was checking for Sadie, and she didn't seem interested. With her head held high, and a distant look on her face, she looked more annoyed than anything. She made her way through the crowd that was now in her face, waving their hands with "hellos" and their immediate wants of attention.

Sadie's arrogance and swagger instantly made Raya's pussy drip with moisture.

Immediately after Sadie climbed out of the car, a petite woman wearing a black miniskirt and six-inch red stilettos hopped out of the passenger side. The crowd blocked Serenity and Raya's view for a moment. But then she reappeared. Her clothing left nothing to the imagination. The little exhibitionist proudly strutted, wearing a sheer blouse, no bra, and her ample breasts with protruding nipples said it all. The lady was on display and had no shame.

The little woman carried two bags in her hands, while Sadie walked along with nothing in her. She toted the bags proudly and followed close behind Sadie, trying not to outstep her.

Sadie was an attractive "stud" female. She lived her life strictly as a man. She was respected by the fellas and lusted after by the women.

The petite woman wasn't masculine like Sadie. She

looked like a short supermodel. Obviously, she was the feminine of the two.

Raya spoke with attitude after the passenger got out. "And that's Tootsie. She's Sadie's main chick, wifey status."

"Sadie, huh? Main chick, huh? She has others that know about Tootsie?" Serenity asked.

"Hell, yeah! Shit, it don't even matter to her. She does what she does."

"Well, I guess women can have their cake and eat it too!" Serenity laughed.

"Don't laugh. Didn't you see that crowd? That car?" Raya spat back as if Serenity said something out of place.

"How did she get a car like that, anyway?" Serenity asked, trying to redeem herself from her last comment. She only saw cars like that at fancy car shows or in magazines like *Hemmings Sports & Exotic Car* magazine.

"Sadie is Shawn P's little sister. Did you not do your remedial class in 'Socially Cool' before you got here? You didn't go to Twitter, FB, MySpace . . . Do I really have to name them all?" Raya asked in amazement.

"Okay, okay, so I didn't do my homework on the elite and most popular people. I just knew my man was on the football team. And whoever was hanging with him, I would eventually get to know. So, tell me, who's Shawn P?" Serenity asked, not knowing who the hell Raya was talking about. *Am I supposed to know these people?* she thought.

"Girl, where the hell have you been? Shawn has been

the biggest boss in D.C. for years. That nigga got paper for days. You'd have to be a millionaire just to keep up with him," Raya said, as if explaining something very important to an ignorant child.

"Word," Serenity said, watching along with everyone else as Sadie disappeared into the building.

"Hell, yeah. He gives his baby sister whatever she wants. She had a Corvette the end of last school year and now she got the Lambo. Who she fooling?" Raya said smiling and clapping her hands together one time like an impressed fan.

"Oh, so her brother gives her anything, huh? How old is Sadie, and where she stay at? 'Cause I ain't seen her 'til now, and I have been here for a minute," Serenity lied, not wanting to reveal her embarrassment. She picked up her bag.

"Don't tell me you interested in her. Let me find out you curious, Serenity," Raya smiled, reaching for Serenity.

"What you reaching for? I gots nothing for you," Serenity responded quickly so Raya would get off the subject and stop making it seem like she was paying attention to another female. She tried not to seem attracted, but her roommate's panties weren't the only wet ones. Serenity was thrown off by the instant attraction, and she knew that she was definitely curious now.

Raya knew not to force the issue so she followed suit and stood up. She grabbed her bag as a tall, slender, Hispanic woman approached her with a big Kool-Aid smile.

"What's up, Raya?" she asked while looking seductively toward Serenity.

"What's good, girl?" Raya replied, knowing why her smile was so wide.

Serenity glanced at the appealing woman. Then she quickly reached into her bag for something—anything—avoiding more eye contact, indicating that she had no interest in the woman or her conversation.

"Not much. Who's this fresh meat?" she motioned her head toward Serenity while twirling her tongue around the lollipop in her mouth.

"Oh, sorry, girl. How rude of me. This is my roommate Serenity. Serenity, this is Brooklyn," Raya said, staring at Brooklyn and remembering their hot and heavy episode last year.

"Yeah? What's up? Let me be straight with you; it ain't that type of party," Serenity said, quickly shutting down any wrong notion that Brooklyn might of had about her.

"My bad, my bad," Brooklyn said, playfully backing away with her hands up in the air. She smiled, and her eyes never left Serenity's ass. Her jeans were so tight they looked like they were painted on. Serenity's plump, juicy ass was displayed for all to see.

Raya laughed, watching Brooklyn practically drooling over Serenity. She knew Brooklyn through the lesbian community that the students formed. Everyone who was a candy licker knew each other on campus.

Brooklyn focused her attention back to Raya. "So

you going to Sadie's Pajama Bash next weekend?" she asked.

"Oh, shit. It's next weekend? Hell, yeah, I'm going. It's the biggest party of the year! You know 'us ladies' can't miss all that free skin that's gonna be thrown around. You remember what happened last year, don't you?" Raya asked, her excitement building.

"Yeah, that shit was the bomb. I think that was the best time I ever had with so many women," Brooklyn said, grinning lustfully from ear to ear.

"Yeah, girl," Raya responded with laughter and slapped her a high five.

"Cool. Then I'll see you there," Brooklyn said, smiling and turning toward Serenity. "I hope to see you there too, ma," she added, staring at Serenity, she then walked off, almost stumbling because she couldn't tear her eyes away from Serenity's sexy ass.

"What's her deal? You betta let ol' girl know that I don't swing that way," Serenity said to Raya as she watched Brooklyn almost bust her ass entering the building.

"Don't pay her no mind. Every girl is fair game for her. That bitch is crazy like that," Raya said, brushing it off.

"So what's this party I'm hearing about? I've seen the poster about it all over campus for the past week."

"It's a big party that Sadie's been throwing ever since she began going to school here. It's going on three years now. It's a masquerade party. You know, where everyone wears a mask. I don't think this is your type of party though," Raya said with a sly smile.

By Raya's coy look, Serenity got the hint that it was a rainbow-ticketed affair. "I think I'll pass," Serenity said, turning to walk into the building to her next scheduled class.

"Whatever. But, believe me, you will *want* to be there. I *know* I'm gonna be there. It goes down at those parties. You don't have to stay for the afterparty. Just come to the party," Raya announced. "I'll catch up with you later. I'ma be late for class."

"Later," Serenity said, walking toward the entrance of the building with the masquerade party heavy on her mind. *What if I went? It's not like anyone would notice me. I'd have on a mask.*

With thoughts of this infamous party bouncing around in her brain, Serenity wasn't paying attention to her steps. Suddenly, she bumped into Sadie, knocking her shades to the floor. Serenity quickly blinked. She couldn't believe what she had just done.

Sadie looked down at Serenity. Serenity's striking sea-green eyes immediately captured her attention.

"I'm so sorry. Are your glasses broken or scratched?" Serenity asked, cursing herself silently.

"Um . . . I don't know. Don't worry about that. I got another pair in the car," Sadie replied, quickly overcoming her delayed response.

Serenity couldn't believe how much of an attraction she felt toward this woman. Sadie's smell was even like a man's. Her face was more beautiful up close than she had previously thought. Her eyebrows were perfectly arched over her eyes. Her lips looked juicy enough to kiss. Her dark sun-tanned skin showed no imperfections on her face. She backed away quickly and said, "What? You caught a two-for-one special?"

Sadie laughed and answered, "Something like that, yeah."

"Well, if I need to replace them, let me know 'cause I got only about a note on me now. I'd have to go the bank," Serenity said causally.

"Shorty . . . I mean . . . um . . . what's your name?" Sadie didn't want to blow this encounter.

"Serenity, and yours?" she asked, even though she already knew.

"I'm Sadie. Listen . . . Serenity. . . ." She inched closer, "That little accident was all my fault; don't worry 'bout the glasses. They can be replaced." She assured her no damage was done.

Serenity's phone started to ring. "I better get this. It's my man. Nice meeting you. I'll see you around." She turned and walked away to answer her phone.

Sadie stood there and watched Serenity's shapely ass walk away. She was totally mesmerized by the sound of Serenity's voice and her looks. She needed to know everything about her—immediately.

Serenity lay in bed, pretending to be asleep, as usual. Then she heard Raya and another voice that sounded familiar. It was Brooklyn, the slender Hispanic woman she met a few days ago. They were trying so hard not to make any noise to wake her.

Soon, she heard Brooklyn softly asking Raya, "Baby, is my pussy wet? You ready to cum for me? You gonna rub your hot pussy while you lick my sweet candy, baby?"

They were making love just a couple of feet away from her. The sounds of tongues slurping and licking and Brooklyn's pussy bouncing up and down on Raya's face traveled around the room and screamed in Serenity's ears.

Serenity once again found herself rubbing her clit while only imagining how it felt to taste a female. Thoughts of Sadie's flickering tongue like a snake against her swollen clit turned her on. She pretended her own face was buried in Brooklyn's juicy, succulent pussy. She felt the urge to cum and her legs began to shake. She wanted it. She needed it. And goddamn it, she was gonna get it.

She couldn't help it anymore—she had to have it. Serenity stood up and almost startled the lovers off the twin-sized bed. They instantly stopped sexing and looked at her with blushing faces against the soft light of the room. But they didn't expect what was about to happen next.

Serenity walked over and joined them in the bed.

No one said a word. Her actions spoke a thousand words. Serenity placed her hands on Brooklyn's plump ass and began to massage it hungrily.

At first, Brooklyn jumped with suspicion, but she

quickly relaxed and got into the groove. She enjoyed what was being done to her. She returned to her previous position, on Raya's face, and began to ride it once again. Her ass rotated slowly in the flickering light of the scented candle.

The sight of Raya lustfully stroking her dripping wet flower was driving Serenity crazy. Raya was neatly waxed, showing her thick lips and enlarged clit. Serenity felt as if she were in a trance.

She straddled Raya while Brooklyn was still getting her rocks off. Then she started to grind her hot pussy.

"Oh, Serenity! Yes, baby, come get yours. Fuck me faster, Serenity . . . Fuck me, baby . . . Fuck me like you wanna cum!" Raya screamed out.

Serenity's pussy was now drenched, and her pace began to quicken. She reached for Brooklyn's ass cheeks to spread them apart. The sight of her asshole and Raya's hot box below her pussy surged the freak in her. She slowly stuck her tongue in Brooklyn's asshole and moved it at a rapid pace. Serenity was now fully indulged in a ménage à trois and discovered her freaky side.

This feels like heaven. I can't believe this is happening. It's so good . . . *Serenity thought while continuing to expertly work her tongue on Brooklyn like she had been doing it forever.*

Raya moved into position to give her welcomed bed guest what she really wanted.

Serenity slipped her finger in and out of Brooklyn's wet love box, who began to yell, "I'm cumming . . . I'm cumming . . . Right there . . . Right there . . . That's it . . . I'm cum—" her legs began to shake uncontrollably as her river poured forth.

The sweet liquid slowly dripped onto Serenity's fingers. It rolled inch by inch down her hand. She took her fingers out of Brooklyn and tasted her.

Brooklyn started to lick Serenity's fingers. Their faces got closer, and they kissed passionately as lovers would, their tongues dancing in each other's mouth. Brooklyn took her fingers and delicately circled them around Serenity's hard, stiff nipples.

Raya moved into position to give her welcomed bed guest what she really wanted.

Before Serenity knew it, she was now flat on her back and Brooklyn was sucking on her hard nipples. Raya was now teasing Serenity's clit with her expert tongue. Little by little, she began to lick and suck up Serenity's overflowing nectar as her clit pulsated and beat to a wild rhythm.

The freak was becoming stronger. Serenity signaled to Brooklyn that she wanted her to get a taste with Raya. Brooklyn quickly moved into position and gently swept Raya's hair behind her ears. This can't be happening. If this is how it's gonna be, then I can't wait 'til it happens again, *Serenity thought, giving herself over to the lust consuming her body and mind.*

Raya and Brooklyn's tongues became intertwined with a rapid circular movement on Serenity's now-swollen clit. She gyrated her hips to the rhythm of their tongues. Raya glided her two fingers in and out of Serenity's pussy as fast as she could. She wanted her to cum all over her face with back-to-back climaxes.

After what felt like an eternity of pure orgasms, Serenity signaled to both of them to switch positions. She led Raya to lay down and gazed at her sweetness between her legs. Brooklyn easily slid behind Serenity to triple the pleasure.

Now Serenity slipped down and began to lick Raya's hot love box. She stuck two fingers inside her pussy, somehow knowing exactly how to please her. Then Serenity pressed her face deeper into Raya's hot, wet pussy.

"Yeah, baby, eat that pussy . . . damn, that feels so good . . . you like eating pussy, don't you, baby? This pussy loves you," Raya yelled out in ecstasy.

Serenity quickly found her G-spot. Who knows how to find a woman's G-spot better than another woman? *Serenity played with the thought. Brooklyn continued to eat her pussy from behind.*

The sex brought her a newly discovered high for free. She shook her ass like Jell-O, wanting more.

Raya kept grinding her hips in a slow, circular motion as her lips quivered in ecstasy. She screamed in pleasure, "Here it comes, baby . . . I'm gonna cum . . . Please, Serenity, don't stop . . . Whatever you fuckin' do, don't stop."

Serenity sucked on Raya's clit harder, making her shudder continuously.

Brooklyn took her cue from Raya. She slid her fingers feverishly into Serenity's love box as she moved her tongue in and out of her butt hole as quickly as she could. She felt Serenity's walls tightening around her fingers. Serenity was on the verge of climaxing.

Serenity felt her nut cumming and pumped furiously into Brooklyn's face. She grabbed hold of Raya's tit and twisted her nipples. She then looked at Brooklyn's luscious berry and entered it with her fingers. The wet, warm touch of Brooklyn's flesh against her fingers made her want to cum even harder. "Oh, shit . . . Right there . . . Yeah, right there . . . make me cum! Fuck me, baby!" Serenity screamed as her legs began to wobble in an uncontainable wave of sexual frenzy. She felt so good, and finally, she was satisfied.

Serenity woke up with her panties and inner thighs soaked. Her hand was still on her warm clit. She was masturbating in her sleep and didn't even know it. She sat up and looked across the room.

Raya was sound asleep with Brooklyn alongside her.

"That was too real," Serenity whispered as she felt a light orgasm vibrate through her. She tensed up and quietly slid out of bed to take a shower. Her curiosity was getting the best of her. She became aware of it more and more. She shook her head and whispered, "I gotta stop this. This is only a phase that every young woman goes through in life. I just gotta spend more time with Rock to battle the fantasies."

Chapter Three

Rock and Serenity were sitting front-row center at the men's basketball game cheering their home team on. The building was packed for the season opening game. The place was definitely jumping, and the energy was at its pinnacle. The home team was winning, and it was approaching halftime.

"I'm about to go get something to drink. Do you want something, baby?" Serenity asked, trying to beat the crowd to the concession stands.

"Yeah . . . yeah, bring me back a coke," Rock said with annoyance in his voice at being interrupted from paying attention to the game.

Serenity stood up, and when she did, most of the males' eyes around her shot instantaneously to her backside. Her tight Baby Phat low-rise jeans and her home team's jersey tightly pulled into a neat knot just above her belly button demanded attention from everyone within eyesight who had a dick. But it also caught the eye of someone with a slit—Sadie.

Sadie observed Serenity walking toward the hallway that led to the concession stands. Her mouth became dry at the sight of her. She quickly tapped the shoulders of the woman sitting in front of her and leaned in to whisper, "Hey, baby, can we have some fun with her?" The woman's face turned slightly to the right, guided by Sadie's gentle touch. "I want you to taste that right in front of me. Let's see if you can make it happen," Sadie softly spoke into the young woman's ear while slowly massaging the middle of her back.

The woman instantly stood up as if Sadie just recharged her battery and headed in the direction of Serenity.

Sadie saw something she liked and most of the time if she wanted something, she usually got it—no matter how inconceivable it might seem. She smiled as she watched Serenity's ass sway back and forth until she disappeared into the hallway. "That's going to be my bitch," she confidently said to her entourage.

Rock felt his phone vibrate. "Hey, Iris, what's up?"

"When am I gonna be able to see you?" she said irritated.

"Let's get up sometime later. I'm with Serenity," he said looking around.

"Yeah, a'ight. One." Iris hung up the phone quickly.

Rock removed the phone from his ear and looked at the screen. *What the fuck did I say? Damn*, he thought.

He pulled her number back up and decided to send her a text.

U hung up. U know wat up. Don't act like that. Talk later.

Rock placed his phone back on his hip.

"Can I have a medium popcorn and two cokes, please?" Serenity asked the vendor and slipped her finger into her back pocket to retrieve her money. As soon as she reached for the money, she felt a gentle hand pat her behind. She grew a quick attitude and turned around immediately, ready to cuss out the nigga who disrespected her. But to her shock, it wasn't a man at all; it was Tootsie. *Sadie must be here*, Serenity smiled at the thought.

"Hey, there, beautiful," Tootsie said, twirling the red, cherry lollipop around in her mouth.

"You barking up the wrong tree, ma! Back the fuck up before you get hurt by this bitch for disrespecting me the way you did!" Serenity barked, moving to the side in case this chick was ready to call her bluff.

"That's not what my radar is telling me," Tootsie said, stepping closer to Serenity and closing the gap of their personal space.

Now standing nearly toe to toe with her, Serenity put her hand up, touching Tootsie's chest, trying to block her from getting any closer.

"Your mouth says no, but your eyes say something totally different. If I'm wrong, please excuse me, but it's written all over your face. I peeped the way you been watching Sadie around campus. How you get all tense and shit once she enters a room. That's *exactly* why I'm stepping to you on her behalf. She wants me to personally invite you to her party on Saturday. She said she wants to get to know you." Tootsie edged closer to her and gave her lollipop a slow lick. "Up close and personal."

"I'm good. I don't swing that way. I already know how y'all get down," Serenity said, turning her back on Tootsie and retrieving her order off the countertop.

"Suit yourself. But that offer is always open for you, sweetie," Tootsie offered, walking off and purposely rubbing up against Serenity's backside again.

Serenity wanted to curse her ass out and stomp the bitch to the floor after Tootsie's last attempt to entice her. But she kind of liked the way it felt to be flirted with by a woman. She walked away with the popcorn and drinks and returned to her seat alongside Rock. Settled, she scanned the faces of fans and caught Sadie looking at her. She felt butterflies in her stomach.

Sadie was looking so sexy with her Cartier glasses on and her fresh haircut.

Serenity locked eyes with Sadie, and neither of them looked away. It was only a split second, but to her, it felt like an eternity. She finally looked away and kissed Rock on the cheek just to let Sadie know that she wasn't interested. She had to admit though, she was attractive as hell. *What the hell is wrong with me? Am I gay? Why in the world am I actually feeling this chick?* she questioned herself. There were so many questions, but she had no answers. She pretended to watch the game, but that was the last thing on her mind.

Sadie Smith was all she thought about, and she had to confess she was curious to learn more about her.

On the way home, Rock noticed Serenity was quiet so he decided to see what was on her mind. "You good, ma? You haven't really said a word since you came back from the concession stands." He reached over and ran his fingers through her hair.

"I'm good, Rock. Just was thinking about something, that's all," she said, feeling her pussy getting wet just thinking about being pleasured by Sadie. She couldn't fight the urge and the images that kept popping up in her mind.

Rock looked at her tight body, and his manhood began to grow inside of his jeans. The only thing on his mind at that point was seeing his woman naked. "Want to go back to my place?" he asked, placing his hand on her lap.

"Yeah, that's cool," Serenity said nonchalantly.

She couldn't stop thinking about Sadie. No matter how hard she tried to tell herself that she wasn't curious, the urge was getting stronger and stronger by the day. Sadie Smith was number one on her list. She had to admit it, she had a crush on a woman for the first time.

Rock and Serenity were back at his apartment, and it didn't take long before the clothes started coming off. He whispered in her ear, "I have a special surprise for you. Just lay back and take those panties off."

Serenity couldn't get her panties off fast enough at the thought of him actually tasting her flower. She had a huge smile across her face. "Baby, you want it like that?" she spoke in a sexy, low tone.

"Yeah, baby, I want it like that . . . Come here." Rock grabbed her and laid her on the sofa. She lay there with not a stitch of clothing on. He parted her legs widely and buried his face in her juices. Then he lightly pinched her nipples. She squirmed in pleasure as she looked down at his neatly waved hair as he pushed his head deeper into her crotch.

"Ahh . . . right there . . . that's right, baby . . . lick my sweet pussy, daddy . . ." she moaned in a low voice. A moment later, she cringed when he became too rough, but she didn't say anything. She wanted to get hers this time around. With her eyes closed, she began to imagine that it was Sadie going down on her, rather than Rock. She arched her back and maneuvered his aggressive tongue to the right spot and the foreplay got even better.

Rock noticed her unusual freakiness and got arrogant. *I must really be doing my motherfuckin' thing today*, he thought. He stood up and dropped his pants. His ten inches stuck straight out and saluted her. He started to stroke it while looking at her dripping love box. Then Rock got on his knees with his pipe in hand ready to put in work. He rubbed his swollen tip on her pulsating clit and began to play with it.

"That feels good, Rock," she moaned.

Rock couldn't wait any longer, and he plunged his

manhood into her pool of love. "Umm," he grunted, feeling the tight grip of her walls and warm wetness. He began to take deep, long strokes in and out of her, holding her legs well above her head. His ass muscles flexed every time he stroked. His chocolate complexion was the same shade as his pipe, and it looked even darker against her pink insides. Sweat began to drip down. He moved his ass round and round while inside her, going as deep as his pipe would allow.

Serenity held her legs even further back. She felt him deep inside of her, hitting her G-spot. "Yes, daddy . . . fuck me harder, daddy . . . I want to cum all over your dick, baby . . . Ahh, yesss . . ." she screamed in pure bliss. *Yesss, this is what I want! A woman could never give me dick like this!* she thought.

Rock's pumps suddenly became faster and harder. "Yeah, baby . . . this my pussy!"

She knew what time it was. He was about to cum before she even came close. "No, no! Hold on, I gotta get mine! Slow the fuck down, Rock!" she demanded, trying to stop him from going any faster.

"I can't, baby . . . It feels so fuckin' good, baby . . . Here I cum—" he said releasing a walnut-sized glob of semen onto her stomach as he pulled out. His pole instantly went limp, and he fell to the floor exhausted, breathing heavily and sweating like a madman. He looked over at her and saw a disappointed look on her face. Finally, Rock stood up and moved next to Serenity on the sofa. "So, you liked that, huh?" he said, trying to find out if his surprise totally flipped her wig.

She smacked her lips in dissatisfaction. *This nigga always does this shit. As soon as it gets to feeling real fuckin' good, he knocks himself out of the race.* She rolled her eyes and pushed him away.

Rock lay on his back and stared up at the ceiling with a silly grin on his face.

Serenity climbed on top of him and grabbed his dick. She stroked it to make it grow.

Wow, she wants it again?

"Come on, Rock. I want to cum too. What the fuck? Am I fuckin' with a two-minute nigga?" she said. She rubbed his tip against her wetness, but still didn't get any response.

"Why don't you give me five minutes?" he pleaded, slapping her ass. He didn't want her to notice he was embarrassed by her rant. He always came too quickly with her, and he knew it. *Lately, she notices it more and more. But I can't tell her that since she ain't giving me what I want . . . I gotta get it elsewhere.*

Annoyed with his shortcomings, Serenity jumped off him and headed to the shower.

He watched her round ass shake from side to side. *Why won't she just give in?* He sat there in thought. A moment later, he stood up and picked up his phone from the floor. "Yo', wat up?"

"Baby, I was wondering when you were gonna come see me. Sorry about earlier but you just kill me," Iris said.

"Okay, kill me in about an hour," he said smiling.

"The usual spot? First, we gotta get business out the way, and then I could kill you," she laughed.

"Yeah, there's something I want to talk to you about. I know a way that you can have your cake and eat it too. It just may take a little time," Rock spoke softly.

"I already told you I don't want a relationship with you. How many times we gotta go through this. Yes, you are the only guy I have ever been with and you know it's strictly a friendship with benefits. That's it, nothing more. . . . But now that you bring it up, I wouldn't mine tasting your sweet honey, Serenity," she said, knowing he wouldn't deny her the opportunity.

"A'ight, I'll see you in an hour. Bye." Rock removed the phone from his ear and ended the call. *Damn, if I can get what I really want, I'd be the man with two bad-ass bitches at my side.*

Serenity stepped into the shower and turned on the water, letting it hit her body. She was still horny, and Rock left her hanging on a limb—again. She closed her eyes, letting the water splash her face and cascade down her. She couldn't stop thinking about Sadie for some reason. *There's something about her eyes*, she thought, beginning to rub her nipples. Her body began to tingle, and she let her hand slip south, down to her clit. She propped a leg on the soap dish holder and began to rub herself, slipping her finger in and out of her hot, aching pussy. She humped the air pleasing herself. Involuntarily, the name "Sadie" slipped from her lips.

Serenity grabbed her nipples harder and twisted them. The feeling was getting good to her. The water hit her clit on the right spot as she continued. The urge to cum was approaching. She spread her legs wider and moved her fingers faster working her sweet spot. Then she slipped three fingers inside her pussy and threw her head back in intense gratification. Seconds later, her legs began to shake. She squeezed her breast and enjoyed the feeling of a nut—finally. Her juices washed away with the water. She would let Rock slide again.

Finishing up her shower, Serenity tried to remove Sadie from her mind. The itch to experience sex with another woman was growing inside. It was only a matter of time before she stopped holding back.

Serenity sat peacefully in the common area of her dorm. Loud laughter came from the entrance. She looked up and saw Sadie entering. She quickly buried her head behind her textbook.

Sadie walked in and saw Serenity sitting in a quiet corner. She looked nervous.

The laughter distracted the others in the common area.

Sadie walked over to Serenity and sat down. "What you studying, ma?"

"Um . . ." she replied confused. Serenity looked at the book and said, "Introduction to Psychology."

"Do I make you nervous or something?"

"Why you say that? And no, you don't," Serenity smarted off.

"Well, by the way you looked, and the fact that you actually had to look at the book to make sure . . ." Sadie replied smiling. "Did you have dinner yet? We can go get some, if you like."

"Ahh, I don't get down like that. Like I told your friend. Yeah, and don't have none of your friends get all up in my face again. That shit was *not* cool," she quickly added.

"Look, ma, all I asked was if you ate yet. 'Cuz I know I'm hungry as hell. No need for the hostility. Okay, ma? I mean, Ms. Serenity White." Sadie spoke in a low tone.

"Listen, I'm just not that way. Understand? Or do I need to do something about it?" Serenity said, standing up to make her point clear.

"All right, all right, no need for all that. It's cool. We cool." Sadie stood up and walked away grinning.

Serenity was not pleased. She also didn't remember telling her her last name.

Chapter Four

Sadie's crib was a two-story, solid brick house with a two-car garage. It had four-bedrooms, three full baths, a well manicured front and backyard, and a playboy-emblem-shaped pool. Her house was about a hot twenty minutes away from school. Her "conquests" and "no-questions-asked bitches" would always find their way to her house. She was never alone unless she wanted to be. Sadie had bitches—from the best to the naughtiest. And she only allowed certain niggas into her house. The "getting money" and "I got it" niggas got in. She would not consent to any man fucking any one of her bitches without her knowing. Every nigga who-ever she had ties with respected her rules.

Sadie was known by everyone for always getting the woman of every man's dreams on and off campus. It was a big game to her. It was so easy to spend some money, give up some drugs, spend a few nights with some hot, sexy bitches, pleasing their every sexual fantasy. She would hook, line, and sinker those chicks who were sexually deprived. Those who were just confused and wanted to stray were easy pickings. The game was: get the bitch, get more respect.

Pimping was not her game, but everybody who was anybody could always hit her up if they needed some chicks for a party—straight or gay. Many of the females on campus knew her, and they all wanted to be with her. They heard about the wild sex parties and how orgasmic they could be. Sadie's social scene was full of women, drugs, and sex—anytime she wanted.

Sadie took a deep pull of the blunt and held the smoke in her lungs before she released it into the air. Tootsie stood behind massaging her shoulders. She sat in her living room on her thronelike plush white leather chair and smoked a blunt. She watched some of her friends through her glass patio French doors. They were relaxing and talking by the pool. "So, what's with ol' girl at the game? What she say when you stepped to her?" Sadie asked calmly, keeping her eyes glued on the bikini-clad women by the pool.

"I don't think she gets down like that. She acted like I was talking a different language or something when I approached her. She told me to keep it moving."

"Is that right?" Sadie asked smiling and took another deep pull off the blunt.

"Yeah, I think she fuck with that nigga, Rock. You know, the one that's on the football team. I also think he fuck with your brother on the low with some hustling shit. Why don't you ask your brother?" Tootsie suggested, knowing it would irk Sadie. She continued to massage Sadie's shoulders.

"What you mean by that? *Ask my brother?* He don't run shit around here. I know who the fuck that nigga is!" Sadie stood up and shouted at her. "Even if he does have some shit with my brother, he ain't no fuckin' body. Please, you getting me upset."

"Damn, daddy, I didn't mean it like that . . . I just thought . . . Come on, daddy, sit back down, and let me please you. Tell me what you need from me," Tootsie said seductively while removing the top of her black, thong bikini.

Sadie smiled and sat back on her throne. Her shoulders were once again being massaged. "Yeah, I know ol' dude. Fuck him though. I need this shorty, ASAP. I see the way she looks at me. Trust me, baby girl, eyes do not lie. I want you to press her for me, ya know? Get her used to having a woman push up on her. Then that's when I'ma step to her and—" She inhaled deeply and released circles of smoke into the air. "Game over," she said arrogantly, putting out the blunt. She grabbed Tootsie's breasts and said, "Kiss daddy, baby girl!"

"Daddy, can I ask you why you want her? Do you not want me anymore?" Tootsie stood up and removed her thong.

Sadie grabbed her by the hips and moved her closer. Tootsie's belly button was now inches from Sadie's face. She slipped her tongue in and out of her belly button and glided her fingers over Tootsie's wet, pulsating opening.

Tootsie started to moan, knowing she wouldn't get an answer, at least not now.

They began to kiss, and within minutes, the other four chicks peeked that the party had started. They hurried inside to join in the fun.

Sadie was about to get her daily orgy on, but the only person she wanted to taste was Serenity.

"Now that everyone's here, let's get this shit poppin'! Ya know what I mean!" Sadie smiled and reached for another blunt off her coffee table. Then she sat back comfortably in her chair, lit her blunt, and released big clouds of smoke into the air.

Sadie looked at the women surrounding her. Then her eyes zeroed in on Tootsie's crotch, and she licked her lips. "Show me what you got, baby," she said hungrily.

Tootsie sat on the coffee table directly in front of Sadie with her legs spread open as wide as they could go, exposing her bald, sweet berry.

Sadie licked her lips again, smiling with pure lust. She couldn't take her eyes off the prize. She glanced at the other women, also engaging in some form of sexual activity. Sadie was what you called a nymphomaniac. Her sexual appetite was major, and she needed it satisfied all the time. Her enormous collection of sex toys were placed strategically throughout the house. The sex could happen anywhere and at any time. She believed in being prepared.

Tootsie used her two fingers to play with herself, putting a show on for her "daddy."

"Just like that, baby . . . Yeah, play with that pussy for daddy . . ." Sadie whispered, dipping her head down to taste the flowing honey. She gently rubbed against Tootsie's swollen clit. Sitting back, she relit her blunt, inhaled deeply, and continued to watch the orgy taking place in the room. *If she'd just give me a chance . . . just once*, she thought about Serenity.

"Ahh . . . ahh . . . yes, yes, yesss . . ." a caramel-skinned female hollered, reaching for the female closest to her with the biggest ass. "Come here, sweetheart. I want my face in that pussy when I cum . . ." She looked down at the light-skinned chick eating her and continued, "Keep sucking that clit, baby . . . I'm gonna cum . . ." The caramel chick parted her pink lips so her little man could be fully exposed. Then she grabbed the chick's head working her and made her suck her swollen clit like a lollipop, moving her head up and down, licking and flicking. "That's it, sweetie, back that prime ass up . . ." She rubbed her fingers against the chocolate woman's enlarged clit. "Yeah, you feel that . . . you like that, don't you . . ." she whispered, teasing her fat, juicy ass with her tongue as she inserted a dildo into the woman's throbbing, wet pussy.

"Yes, fuck that pussy, bitch . . . You like sucking on this pink, fat pussy . . . Yeah, hit that spot . . . make me cum, bitch . . ." the chocolate, fat-ass female screamed in lust-filled pleasure.

Sadie was snapped out of her thoughts of Serenity by

the screams of ecstasy of the other females. She motioned to the bronze-skinned Hispanic female seated on the opposite sofa to open her legs wider and play with herself.

The Latin chick did as she was told. She lay back on the sofa, placing one foot on its highest point. Then she grabbed her other leg and held it behind. Slowly her fingers moved in and out of her moistness. She stared lustfully at Sadie and pushed her fingers in deeper, deliberately, moaning softly.

Sadie licked her lips and motioned her to come closer.

The woman stood up and approached. She was ready for her turn to play.

Tootsie continued to expose her shaved, hot, titillating, and purring kitty. She got off when Sadie played with company.

Sadie whispered to the Latin chick, "I want you to use that tongue wherever I point my finger on her body, okay?" She began to play with Tootsie, indirectly. Sadie pointed at Tootsie's breasts, then along her stomach, then right on her pelvic bone, and finally, her inner thighs. Hot, she stood up and told Tootsie to lay down on the coffee table. Her legs were spread wide enough to hang off the edge. Sadie then told the Hispanic, "Taste her, sweetie . . . Tell me how she tastes . . ."

The Latin woman started to run her fingers over Tootsie's erect nipples in a circular motion. Then she bowed her head to ravish the pink sweetness in front of her.

"You want this for daddy, right baby . . . you want me to be happy, don't you, baby?" Sadie asked in a low, sexy tone.

"Yes, daddy, please, daddy . . . I want what you want . . ." Tootsie moaned while her clit was expertly sucked and licked.

"I want her, baby . . . I want to watch you please her . . ." she slipped her wet tongue in Tootsie's ear and continued. "You want her too, right, baby? Tell me you want her, baby . . ."

Sadie stood up and dropped her swimming trunks, exposing her hairless pussy. She motioned to the Hispanic to move aside. She picked up Tootsie, walked toward the other side of the room, and dropped her on the lounge chair. Then she climbed on top of her, strategically putting her large clit directly on Tootsie's wetness. They both were extremely moist and burning hot. Sadie stroked Tootsie's sweet spot as if she had the firm, stiff cock of a man. Slowly, seductively, she moved one of her fingers in and out of Tootsie's mouth.

Tootsie moaned and sucked it like it was her daddy's big, hard strap-on.

Sadie's grind came faster on her. She bent her head slightly closer and said, "Tell daddy, baby . . . I want to hear it."

Tootsie didn't want it to stop. She relished in the luxury and her top-notch benefits. She gave in. "Yes, daddy . . . I want her . . . I want to taste her . . . mmm . . . You think she's sweet, daddy . . . I could taste her, baby . . . mmm . . ." She grabbed Sadie's ass to make her grind against her harder.

"Say her name, baby . . . Who you want your daddy to fuck?" Sadie grabbed Tootsie's legs and held them back so her feet would be touching the wall. She plunged her tongue deep into Tootsie's inviting pink, soaking wet pussy, and eagerly pleased her desires.

"Daddy . . ." she moaned in pleasure, feeling fingers entering her asshole. She pinched on her own nipples and pushed Sadie's head deeper into her hot flesh between her legs. She wanted Sadie to be happy. "Serenity, baby . . . Daddy, I want you to fuck Serenity! Yes, daddy, I want Serenity to cum all over you . . ." her legs shook in waves.

"Yes, baby . . . I like it when you please your daddy," Sadie said, continuing to gently tap on Tootsie's clit, watching her climax again. "Come on, I want to go join the rest of the party. I want you to cum all over these bitches' faces while I fuck them."

Sadie slowly walked back to the other side of the room where things were still poppin'. Then she dipped quickly into an adjacent spare bedroom to grab a couple of her favorite toys. She returned smiling, wearing a huge, black strap-on and holding a long, pink dildo with heads on both ends, and a small vibrator. "Who's gonna give daddy a show?" Sadie asked and instantly her huge strap-on was being sucked and directed into an open wet hole and the toys became friends with their temporary owners. She intensely pounded on some hot flesh, pulling the chick's hair, and smacking her round, voluptuous ass.

Tootsie moved into position and used her hand to expose her ripe, hungry clit.

Sadie's thrusts became deeper and slower. She spoke softly, "Let her taste daddy's berry . . . and make you cum for me . . ." She felt the pleasure of her asshole being licked.

"You heard daddy, taste this sweetness . . . Does it look good, daddy? You like it, baby? Fuck her, daddy, fuck her harder . . . fuck her like she's—" Tootsie was cut short. Her mouth was led to someone's succulent opening being fucked by a vibrator and licked by two intertwining, pierced tongues. The room filled with screams and moans of pure, unadulterated, lust-driven sex. Sadie closed her eyes to picture Serenity that she was fucking.

Before the night was over, everyone in the house had experienced multiple orgasms.

It was the night of Sadie's big bash. She had a precelebration with her entourage at her house. Of course she wanted a little taste before anyone else got some. She was pleased three times over and her special VIP guests were all in awe of her sexual drive and her understanding of how to satisfy the intimate needs of all the women surrounding her.

Serenity contemplated going to the most legendary and notorious party of the year. She actually had not even thought of going 'til she saw Sadie at her dorm's common area. The very next day, she had walked into her room to find a black envelope lying on her pillow. Her named was spelled out in rhinestones and a red lollipop was placed beside it. She pulled out the invitation which, after reading it, she hid under her mattress. She sure as hell did not want Raya to find out about her little run-in with Tootsie or Sadie.

Damn, if I don't go, I just might not ever get the chance again! Well, I know I'm not gay; she won't affect me. To see other women grinding on each other like it was nothing, who cares, but damn, what if I bump into her . . . Should I go for it? Serenity couldn't understand why her love box got so wet when Sadie popped into her mind.

The sounds of Aaliyah serenaded the private club and the place was packed. Half-naked males and females were in attendance rocking their best nighttime attire, dancing with one another.

Raya was wearing a short, black, sheer Victoria's Secret teddy and matching thong. Her black, open-toed, four-inch, "fuck me" pumps showed off her long, slender, glistening legs that were ready to be parted. She was dancing with a few women she knew from last year. Their masks gave their identities away. The regulars never changed their masks for this event.

She'd been attending for a few years. Her older sister, Iris, used to throw these parties too, but they weren't so out there. It was more on the low when it first started.

But it had become crazier every year. After a couple of years, Raya and the others got to know who the regulars were. It was their way of scoping through the women to find new prospects for their midnight snack. There was no way Raya was going for last year's same ole treats when there was a new variety of sweet candy up for tasting.

She thought she recognized someone standing toward the exit door wearing the same pair of pink slippers Serenity wore around the dormitory. *So, she is curious!* she thought, shaking her head in dismissal—Raya was never that lucky to have consistent pussy; not to mention newly turned out virgin pussy. She was sure she left Serenity asleep back at the dorm. But once she got closer, she saw that it was indeed the same pink slippers with the butterfly broach pinned to them. She knew it wasn't time to confront her now and find out who the real person was under that rhinestone-embellished mask. *This bitch couldn't let a ho know nothin'! Damn, and I definitely could have answered all her curiosities about the sweeter side of life. Fuck me!* Raya glanced at her watch. *It's only ten o'clock. Well, let's see what Miss "I Don't Rock That Way" gets into tonight! This will be easier than I thought.*

Raya continued to spy on Serenity from afar, watching her every move.

When she had arrived earlier, Serenity slowly walked to the front of the club. She noticed most people were standing back and watching those who entered. She didn't realize the regulars were scanning the crowd for the sexy, hot newcomers, and the ones who only look good in the dark—male or female. She wanted to prove to herself that she was not gay and her suppressed bi-curious issues were going to be confronted face-to-face tonight, and would leave her *straight.*

She arrived at the front of the entrance line, showed her invitation to security, and entered through the doors feeling beaming eyes at the back of her head. She quickly entered into the safety of the darkness to place her mask on. Spotting an exit, she made her way in that direction just in case her face-to-face confrontation got the better of her. What she didn't know was her mask was one of a kind. It was made specifically for her . . . from Sadie.

Serenity was surprised that an all-out orgy-fest wasn't taking place in the middle of the dance floor. She expected all types of candy lickers to be in attendance. She was pleasantly surprised that there were males and females just having fun. They weren't grinding and humping each other like bitches in heat as she had expected. She finally began to relax as she headed toward the bathroom. There she pulled out her cell phone and dialed Rock's cell number; it went straight to voice mail. *He told me he was going to his boy's house. Why isn't he picking up? Damn!* Serenity pressed the END button without leaving a message.

Rock lay back on his bed with his stiff cock deep in her throat. His fingers fondled the breast of another while lusty moans echoed through the room. He felt his cell phone vibrate on the bed and looked at the caller ID. It read: My Love. He tapped the screen to ignore the call, then tossed the phone onto his lounge chair.

Rock watched as two of the women were deeply interlocked in the sixty-nine position. He watched them suck, lick, and use their fingers to please one another. Both climaxed simultaneously. His cock and tongue were now ready to fuck.

One of the women spit into Rock's hand, then guided him to jerk his dick. As he rubbed his throbbing cock and lay his head back, she filled his view and mouth with luscious, tender, juicy pussy. Rock immediately tried to suck nectar out of the fruit that was bouncing up and down on his face. He knew she only tolerated men in the bedroom because it turned her girlfriend on. He also knew she wouldn't let him fuck her.

"You like that pussy . . . Rock?" a sexy voice asked, placing her hot mouth over his entire ten thick inches.

"Yesss . . . mmm . . ." he slapped the tight little ass that was now reaching another orgasm. He suddenly grabbed her light ass and flipped her onto the bed into the doggie-style position. All the ladies were blindsided by his sudden switch. Instantly, he drove his pole deep into her hot, horny, soaking box. He felt her light thrusts as he slipped his finger into her asshole. "Yes, baby . . . fuck me back . . . Throw that ass back . . . yeah . . ."

One of the ladies eased her way to the headboard of the bed and sat there with her legs open wide as she played with her clit. She got more turned on by seeing her girlfriend getting fucked by a nigga.

Rock palmed each ass cheek of the featherweight and began to slam her down, nice and hard on his unyielding, strong manhood.

"Yeah . . . baby . . . fuck this pussy the way you want it . . . Yeah . . . baby, fuck me hard . . . ram your stiff, big cock into my tiny pussy . . ." the featherweight screamed, moving her fingers swiftly in and out of the pink flesh facing her.

Rock entertained the idea of fucking her tight asshole but set aside the thought as he felt a warm, wet mouth on his balls. His pace picked up speed as she sucked and licked his sack. "Yeah, put both of them in your mouth . . . ahh . . . ahh . . . I'ma 'bout to—" he quickly slipped his dick out and flipped featherweight onto her back. Then he stood up with one hand over his head gripping the ceiling and the other hand jerking his dick.

All three ladies gathered their heads together waiting for his sweet release.

He let loose onto their hungry faces with animalistic pleasure. After each of them tasted every last drop of cum off the tip of his still-firm dick, he wanted to start all over again. But he knew he couldn't contemplate that entertaining thought. He had other business to attend to. He got off the bed with his cock still at full attention and announced he was headed to the shower.

Two of the ladies started to follow behind him with lust still burning in their eyes but were stopped short. "Listen, y'all horny little bitches better lick each other out for a moment and back the fuck up. Remember who allowed you to be here. Don't overstep your boundaries."

He stood in the shower allowing the cascading water to rinse the cum juices off. The bathroom door open. He peeked from behind the shower curtain. "Oh, you came to join me?"

"Yeah, you know I gotta have you for myself sometimes," she said playfully, stepping into the shower.

"Did you do what I asked you to do?" Rock asked with his back to her.

"Yeah, I got my sister to look into it."

"You know she could never find out, right?" he asked, then added, "I just want it to go to a certain point. Don't fuck it up, you hear me?"

"All right, all right, I heard you, just enough to get her peaked," she replied, reaching for his stiff dick.

"Yeah, 'cause I still want to keep fucking you," Rock said, putting her into the doggie-style position.

"You know sometimes I think you got some type of voodoo on me or something." She bent over wanting him.

He gently slid his dick inside her with easy strokes. "Well, maybe it's because I'm the only guy you"—he slammed his dick into her pussy two quick times—"ever fucked . . . mmm . . ."

Serenity moved around the club in a stealthlike manner, not wanting to be noticed. She found a perfect low-key spot on the second floor where she saw everyone entering the club. *Maybe I won't be noticed if I stay up here*, the thought entered her mind as she looked around. *There's nobody here; they're all down there! Perfect. No one will know I'm here watching.* She smiled at the thought, staring into the crowd over the balcony.

"I'm happy you decided to come to my little party." A low voice startled her back to reality.

"Oh, shit!" Serenity practically jumped out of her skin. She turned to hit the person who whispered into her ear unexpectedly. Then she almost stumbled backward over the balcony at the sight of Sadie.

"Hey, you okay? I didn't mean to scare you like that," Sadie said, pulling Serenity closer, preventing her from falling to her death.

Serenity instinctively grabbed onto her savior and buried her face into Sadie's chest. "Whew, I thought I was gonna go over! Shit!" she said relieved. She then flipped the script after her stance became stronger and eased herself off of Sadie. "What the fuck you think you doing, bitch? You could have sent me fuckin' over," she yelled.

"Sorry, ma . . . No need for such foul language. I like to save that for the bedroom," Sadie said with a smile.

Serenity caught a whiff of her cologne, and her pussy tightened. She felt moisture leak onto her panties.

"Will you stay after midnight . . . so I can *really* show you how I can get down?" she said as she reached for Serenity's hand and planted a soft, wet kiss.

"Now, *this* is what I'm talking about," Raya said,

looking at all of the females who were parading past her. Her eyes darted across the room searching for Serenity. *Where are you, my little kitty-cat?* she taunted Serenity in her mind.

Raya walked seductively to the bar to refill her Apple Martini and show her potential prospects her best assets. Her sheer teddy left nothing for the imagination. Her nipples stood at full attention, welcoming any lonely tongue, and her thong signified her plump ass was ready for tossing.

She glanced at her watch again. *Damn, it's eleven-thirty . . . Where are you, my little kitty-cat?* She was just about to give up on the search for Serenity 'til she took an extra shot at the bar. There, her eyes were diverted toward the VIP section on the upper floor. *There you are, my kitty! Oh, no! Damn, that fucking bitch, Sadie. Well, it don't matter what way it's done, but shit, she could fall victim to this bitch. I gotta talk to my sister.* She shook her head and hoped she would still get paid.

Serenity snatched her hand away from Sadie, hoping no one caught their tender moment on camera. "Listen, maybe I'm coming off a little harsh, but I am *not* curious and do *not* like pussy, straight-up. I love hard, firm cock from my man," she protested, stepping away.

Sadie smiled at the challenge. She tapped her shoulder and leaned in close as she whispered, "Yes, you do. You just don't know it yet. I see the way you look at me, baby girl. Eyes never lie," Sadie said with a smooth croon from the pages of a pimp's manual. "See you at midnight," she whispered confidently. She turned her back toward Serenity and walked away.

Serenity felt her warm breath and her soft, smooth lips against her earlobe. A wave of pleasure soared through her body. The wave was now hovering at clitoris level. She wanted to see what really went down after midnight. *I just want to fuckin' watch, not jump into the fire. Well, maybe I do. Damn!*

"It's fuckin' hot in this bitch," Raya said to the cute bartender. She fanned herself trying to prevent the sweat emerging from her brows. She thought she wore the perfect freak 'em outfit. She forgot how jam-packed and steamy this party could get from all the niggas. It never failed. Some nigga always tried to stay around for the true freaks to show out.

She glanced at her watch. It was minutes to midnight. She scanned the balcony for Serenity but couldn't see her.

Sadie, however, was donned in a cocaine white, plush Yves Saint Laurent terry cloth robe that hung to the floor. She wrapped the tie so tightly you would think she was completely naked under there.

As for Tootsie, she wore a white, lace low-rise thong and a tight, white corset that made her waist impeccably small. It pushed her breasts together, making them easy prey for devouring tongues.

The VIP guests were knocking back shots of Patrón. Sadie looked over the balcony at the sea of women in attendance. She saw Raya standing at the bar. She lifted her shot glass toward her then motioned for her to come up.

Raya declined. She didn't want to seem desperate.

Some women were gathered in the middle of the dance floor. They were nervously looking at their watches, waiting for the clock to strike midnight, waiting anxiously for the DJ to kick the straight females along with their corresponding mates out to the curb.

The female DJ finally got on the mic and announced, "Yo', it's three minutes to midnight, and you know what that means. If you don't have the proper invite, get to steppin', losers . . . It's time to get the fuck out!" she said, making most of the women smile. "Only lesbians and bisexual females allowed from this point on. Newcomers and old, y'all know the rules."

A wave of protests and sighs erupted from the guys, and one man even yelled, "Come on, baby, let me stay and throw some sausage into the mix!" causing everyone to chuckle at his comment.

Raya smiled and looked up at Sadie.

Serenity crept to the bar as the announcement came over the speakers. The shouts of "get your freak on" through the crowd was surreal. *Fuck it! I have only this moment to satisfy my curiosity. And if I ain't with it, then I can just say I was drunk! No, I should just turn around and walk out the fuckin' door! I can't . . . I won't,* thoughts bounced around her mind. She ordered four shots of Patrón.

Chapter Five

An oversized plush mat was placed onto the dance floor as soft music was being played just low enough so that you could still hear the sounds of lesbian sex. The private club was transformed into a haven for ecstasy for one night. The flickering strobe light was the only illumination provided in this sexual escapade.

Sadie stood in the VIP section on the upper floor and looked down at what she created: an all-out female orgy. Over fifty women licking, sucking, fucking each other, and it was a beautiful sight. She looked out at the crowd, searching for someone or something; then she spotted it: the one mask with the signature mark—a glow-in-the-dark playboy bunny symbol over the right eye of the mask. It was her—Serenity—nervously lingering by the exit door, feeling the shots she had just knocked back. Sadie watched her. Serenity seemed to be uncomfortable watching girls suck each other's pussy and getting penetrated with rubber dildos. She smiled, making her way down the stairs followed closely by Tootsie. She couldn't wait to taste Serenity.

Serenity had to pinch herself, thinking she was in a dream. She stood pressed against the wall near the exit door and watched women openly freak each other without a care in the world. After the party was cleared out of its noninvitees, the fun began. Females were exploding off of ecstasy pills, and others were just naturally freaky. She kept telling herself to leave, but she couldn't take her eyes off the scene in front of her.

She watched a string of ten women sexing each other. They formed a human sex chain. Everyone was eating pussy and getting theirs eaten at the same exact time. Serenity's juices started flowing as her eyes hungrily devoured the scene. She watched females grind their ass on other women's faces. She had never seen such acts before. She knew Raya was somewhere in the mix, but she just couldn't recognize her. Everyone was naked and moaning and screaming as they climaxed. It was hard to distinguish who was who with the short flashes of light.

That's when Serenity saw Sadie walking down the stairs with the same woman who approached her at the basketball game.

By now, Serenity was horny as hell and slippery wet. *Why am I feeling this way?* She couldn't take her eyes off Sadie as Sadie moved closer. She didn't realize that Sadie was fast approaching.

Now, Sadie stood in front of her and no words were spoken. Sadie reached for Serenity's breasts and gently rubbed her rock-hard nipples. She smiled and began to tongue kiss her.

Serenity closed her eyes and a small moan was released from her lips. She then felt another set of hands caressing her back and slowly moving down to her ass. It snapped her out of her trance. Seeing that it was Tootsie who was already naked, she showed a slight smile.

"It's okay, it's okay," Sadie whispered, kissing her neck. She slipped her hand under Serenity's tank top to see if she really wanted this to happen.

Serenity wanted to stop them, but her body was dictating otherwise.

Sadie grabbed her hand and led her up to the private office opposite the VIP section. Tootsie followed close behind. She wanted Serenity to remember her first time with a woman, two women.

Serenity was in a dreamlike state and let them guide her up the stairs, with no reservation whatsoever. *What am I doing?* she thought, reaching the top of the stairs. But by now, her clitoris was throbbing and her nipples tingled, longing for Sadie's touch. Finally she would have her first lesbian experience and with Sadie, who she had wanted for so long.

Sadie opened the door and led Serenity to one of the plush leather sofas facing the enormous fish tank in the wall.

Tootsie closed the door. She walked over to Serenity and began kissing the back of her neck.

Sadie dropped her robe. She was completely naked with many tattoos coloring her beautiful body. She dropped to her knees.

Serenity was turned on by all the artwork on Sadie's perfectly toned, muscular body. "I'm not gay," she whispered. Her mouth formed those words, but her body was screaming, "yes you are!" She wanted to push away Sadie's hands, but they felt so good on her skin. Her tank top came off, and Sadie began to gently twist her nipples like doorknobs, sending chills up Serenity's back.

Serenity eased herself out of her pajama pants, awaiting the experienced tongue. She opened her legs wider and closed her eyes and began to rub on her own breasts, bringing them to her mouth and tasting herself. Sadie slowly licked Serenity's throbbing pussy, making love to it.

The new freakiness was beginning to take hold of Serenity.

Tootsie joined in on sucking at her nipple, then thrust her tongue down Serenity's throat.

Serenity could not hold back the moans of ecstasy. She felt an orgasm coming only after a few seconds of the dual action. Her legs began to quiver, and she tried her best to remain standing. She gripped Sadie's head and pushed her face deeper into her wet, virgin hole. She wanted to explode.

Sadie tasted Serenity's squirt of cum. Tootsie motioned that she wanted a taste too.

"Ahh!" Serenity yelled in pure pleasure. The nectar from her peach shot off. She had never in her life experienced that type of orgasm before. Tonight, she experienced the erotic excitement and orgasm that only a ménage à trois could bring.

On cue, Tootsie stood up and walked out of the room, leaving Sadie and Serenity alone.

Serenity had her eyes closed the whole time and when she opened them, it seemed that she was snapped back to reality. Her clitoris was still throbbing, and her heart was racing.

There was silence in the room when Sadie sat down next to her. She spread her legs, exposing her extra large clitoris and rosy pinkness. She took a drink of the champagne that sat on the floor by the sofa, then whispered, "Come ride my face."

Without hesitation, Serenity obeyed. She walked over and straddled Sadie's face, giving her hard thrusts as she pounded her wound against Sadie's inviting mouth. Serenity rode Sadie's face like a cowboy did to his powerful stud until she climaxed again, squirting sweet cum juices for the second time.

Sadie laid Serenity down and walked over to the mahogany desk and retrieved her gym bag off the top. She pulled out a long, black dildo that curved.

Serenity waited in anticipation, spreading her legs open like a pro. She began to play with herself and moan for her next high. Sadie was bringing out the freak that was always deep inside of her.

Sadie stroked the dildo to get it warm before she put it inside of Serenity. She knew exactly how a woman wanted her dick: warm and hard.

With one hand Sadie parted Serenity's vaginal lips, and with the other, she slipped in the ten-inch dildo. She slid it in slow and began a twisting motion. She used her free thumb to play with Serenity's clit and watch Serenity squirm in bliss. She inserted the dildo in just far enough for pleasure and shallow enough to avoid pain. Smiling, she looked at what she had created.

Serenity was dripping and lusting for more. She had turned into a lesbian nymphomaniac.

Sadie went down on her. She worked her tongue like a tornado while steadily pushing the dildo in and out of Serenity's wet, greedy pussy.

"How you like it?" Sadie grunted in between breaths looking at Serenity who was arching her back in an erotic rush as sexual pleasure consumed her body. After Sadie sucked her clit for a few minutes, she flipped her over. At that point, she put aside the dildo and placed her face directly in Serenity's ass crack using both of her hands to spread her plump cheeks. Her tongue darted in and out of Serenity's asshole in a rapid fuck.

Serenity was totally lost on cloud nine, moaning loudly. She threw her ass back onto Sadie's face, experiencing her salad being tossed for the first time. By the end of the night, she'd had more orgasms than she could count. She was officially no longer curious. She craved more. It was the start of many sexual fantasies she would fulfill.

It was also the beginning of the end.

Chapter Six

Sadie pulled out the chair for Serenity and then seated herself.

After weeks of going back and forth on the phone, texts, and coincidently bumping into each other around school, Serenity agreed to let Sadie take her out. They were on top of the Marriott Hotel at a rooftop restaurant. The moonlight was the only light. The setting was simply gorgeous.

Serenity was tickled pink with happiness. The party was nothing she ever expected. She couldn't believe how good she felt. She had been talking on the phone to Sadie every day since the night of the party. She felt funny keeping it a secret from Rock. But she wanted the experience to continue at a distance. She wasn't ready to pledge to the rainbow flag.

"This is beautiful," Serenity said, scooting up to the table.

"Not more beautiful than you," Sadie responded, removing her shades, exposing her hazel eyes.

Serenity had never received a compliment of that nature from a woman. She blushed, not knowing how to take it. "Thanks," she managed to mumble, avoiding eye contact.

"It's a full moon . . . look," Sadie noticed.

"Yeah, it looks pretty," Serenity said enjoying the view.

"What are you going to school for?" Sadie asked, waving the waiter over.

"I want to be a teacher or a psychologist. And you?"

"Film production. I want to be a director. You know, music videos, small sitcoms, stuff like that. Maybe even do movies," she added. "So, did you enjoy my party? Be honest," Sadie asked, waiting for the waiter to pour more wine into her glass.

"Yeah . . . it was different."

"I saw your freak side. You were *definitely* feeling it. You don't have to be ashamed of what took place. Most women are curious about exploring other women's bodies. But it's only a few who act on it and indulge, know what I mean?" she said with smoothness and certainty.

"I never did anything like that before. I mean . . . I always wondered how it felt and thought about it, but I never had the nerve to act on it. I'm not going to lie, I wouldn't mind doing it again."

"Is that right? Maybe I can help you with that," Sadie suggested taking a sip of her wine.

Serenity looked around the restaurant and noticed it was empty. No one else was dining except for them. She tried to change the subject from sex and added, "It's empty in here tonight. I wonder why."

"That's because I had them close it down especially for you. You're special and deserve to be treated like a queen. I can do that," Sadie said smiling and touched her hand. "Better than any man can."

"Wow, really . . . You think so," Serenity said, trying to ignore her arrogance.

"Yes, I can. Believe me, it can happen. Listen, I'm feeling you. Are you feeling the same? I wanna know. We can have a lot of fun. What do you say?" Sadie said confidently.

"Damn, you are pushy, aren't you? I mean, you know I have a boyfriend and I love him. Besides, I'm not gay. Like you said before . . . just curious." Serenity picked up her glass and sipped on the wine.

"Yeah, I know him. He's on the football team, right?" Sadie asked, wanting to scoop Serenity up and move somewhere far away.

"Umm . . . but I do want to satisfy my curiosity. I mean, can you understand why we would have to keep everything on the low?" Serenity asked with thoughts of extreme sexual pleasure. "Rock could never find out that I did this on my own."

"Okay, no pressure. You're in control," Sadie said, contemplating what she could do to have Serenity for herself.

* * *

Hours later, Sadie's Lamborghini raced down the highway.

Serenity stuck her hand out the window, loving the way the wind felt flowing in between her fingers. Her thoughts were on Rock. How was she going to pull this off? She knew she would fuck Sadie again. Now, how in the hell was she gonna keep seeing her without him knowing?

They were going just under a hundred miles per hour. The luxury car seemed to float on the pavement. Sadie took out the expensive champagne that was stashed behind the passenger's seat. She positioned her knee to steady the wheel while popping the cork. Then she extended her arm over to Serenity and told her to "open up." Sadie poured the drink into her mouth. The champagne spilled everywhere, but Serenity didn't care. She finished the bottle.

Serenity was on top of the world. She was having the time of her life. She never felt so free or so liberated before. The subwoofers pumped out the latest hit song from Drake.

Sadie switched from lane to lane, feeling completely outside the law. "Fuck the law," she screamed, making them burst into laughter. Then she rolled down her window and tossed the bottle out, watching it shatter into pieces when it hit the highway. Both of them were past tipsy, and their adrenaline was pumping to the max. Next, Sadie opened the middle console and pulled out a small white baggy.

Serenity's eyes focused on the small package. She knew what it was.

Sadie gave her a glance and a smile. She drove the car with her knees, just long enough for her to empty the contents in between her thumb and pointer finger. She quickly dipped her nose in it and sniffed.

Serenity was taken by surprise by Sadie's actions. And she was really stunned when Sadie held her hand out so that she could take a hit.

"It'll make you feel good," Sadie promised, focusing back on the road.

Serenity was in a spontaneous mood and just went for it. She sniffed the rest of the cocaine from her hand. Then she threw her head back to prevent her nose from running. All of a sudden, her world turned into overdrive. She looked at Sadie with a seductive glance. Suddenly, her nipples and vagina began to tingle. She was surprised at how quickly the drug had an effect. She had never done any type of drugs before, and the only thing she knew was it made her feel *real* good. She began to feel moist between her legs. Sadie knew Serenity was getting aroused by the way she rubbed her hands on her thighs. No time was wasted. She slipped her hand under Serenity's dress, feeling her soaked panties. She was still driving at a high speed, but it only heightened the pleasure. She slipped one finger into Serenity's hot opening and felt her moist warmth.

Serenity slightly slid down in her seat and parted her

legs wider. Her world began to spin, but she still had an insatiable craving for her spot to be stroked.

Sadie took her finger out and placed it into her mouth, just to tease Serenity. She watched as Serenity pulled out her breasts and began to pinch her own nipples. This time, Sadie stuck two fingers inside Serenity. She slowly poked her, searching for the G-spot. She was a perfectionist when it came to finger popping. She had Serenity to the point where her moans became screams and her tongue was moving like she was eating someone's pussy.

It was time to exit the highway and head to the main campus to drop Serenity off. Sadie fingered her all the way to the side entrance of her dorm building. She knew exactly what she was doing. She wanted to leave Serenity hanging, lusting for more. From the looks on Serenity's face and body language, it seemed to be working.

Serenity was so engaged in what Sadie was doing to her she didn't even notice the car stopped. *Damn, was we really driving that fast? Fuck! You mean that's it . . . Oh my God*, she thought.

Sadie stopped the car and removed her hand from Serenity's walls of wetness. "This is your stop, baby," she said, putting her finger in her mouth and sucking on those sweet juices.

Serenity opened her eyes and stump pumped the air, wanting her to keep going. "Wha—what?" she stuttered.

"This is your stop, baby girl. Are we going to finish this up later? I have to go and handle some business now."

“But why? I want it . . . you . . .” Serenity said almost begging. She never wanted a nut so bad in her life.

“Are we going to finish this up later?” Sadie asked again.

“Don’t keep me waiting, okay? Make it sooner than later,” Serenity sighed. She had thought they were heading to a hotel.

“Just think . . . well, why don’t you call me later if you want to hang out. Patience is the key,” Sadie said smoothly, strategically working on her new baby girl like a surgeon would do his patients. She reached over and softly grabbed Serenity’s face and slid her tongue deep into her mouth. Then she circled her tongue with Serenity’s. “See you later, baby,” she said just before hitting a button on her key ring. The passenger door went up into a butterfly style. Serenity reluctantly stepped out of the car, as horny as ever, with Sadie Smith on her mind.

“Well, look who the cat dragged in,” Raya said, sitting up in her bed. She had been waiting to see Serenity. Since the party she noticed that Serenity would be on the phone talking and blushing, but didn’t realize that Sadie was turning Serenity out. She thought that Serenity would be a little more open about her new discoveries. She never got the scoop on her night at the party after all this time. Raya knew it was Sadie.

“Ah, please!” Serenity snapped back. She definitely didn’t want her business to be out there. After Sadie’s party, she decided to pick up some clothes from her dorm and stay at a nearby hotel to avoid Raya’s onslaught of nosy-ass questions. When she returned back to the dorm, Serenity didn't tell her anything. It was none of Raya's business. After all, she could be a spy for Carla.

"Okay, so you not gonna clue me in on what's happening with you or what's this new shit with you and Sadie?" Raya asked with attitude, as if Serenity had been licking *her* clit and now had moved on to greener pastures.

"What do you mean? And who the fuck you think you talking to anyway? You ain't my fucking man or my bitch!" Serenity ranted off.

"Girl, don't give me that bullshit. Act like that if you want to, but I know what's up. I saw you up in VIP talking to Sadie. I know that she's a damn freak. So what up? You down or what?" Raya asked, seeing straight through her bullshit. She wanted to know if she had missed her opportunity to pop Serenity's cherry. Raya also thought about the cash she probably lost. Her sister, Iris, was pissed and wouldn't give her a dime. She knew that Sadie was that skilled in her game to get Serenity. Raya knew she fucked up.

Iris wanted her to ease Serenity into a threesome and peak her curiosity—before Sadie got to her. She was gonna pay Raya $1,500 just to get her interested. But Sadie beat Raya to it.

"Well, since you so fucking nosy . . . It was nothing," Serenity said. "I was drunk. I can't tell you if I had a good time or not. I wish I knew. I should ask *you* how the party was." She tried to be convincing. "Why you think I wasn't here right after? I didn't know what the hell I did. So I laid low for a week. Let the party noise calm down. I was so pissy drunk, who knows what I did. Why you so up in mine, anyway? Why you so fucking interested?" Serenity demanded, sitting down and folding her arms.

"Sadie is fine as hell. You better be careful though. She just might get your bi-ass to show out. She can make any straight chick turn. It's like turning on the lights for her. It's that easy, trust me," Raya said, wishing that it was her instead of Sadie. She always liked Sadie, but she did her wrong. Like most of the lesbians on campus, Raya got fucked and dumped.

"Yeah, tell me about it," Serenity said sarcastically. She wanted to jump out of her skin thinking about what Sadie's magic fingers had just done. She got up and went to the bathroom to shower. "Damn, if this is how my semesters will be, then I don't think I ever wanna stop going to school," Serenity whispered to herself, heading down the hallway.

"Hey, sis, what's up?" Serenity picked up her phone after getting out of the shower.

"Yo', what up with you? I haven't heard from you and wanted to make sure you were okay," Carla said.

"What you mean? You heard something about me already? Damn, you still can't let go, can you?" Serenity snapped back.

"Huh? . . . Yo', calm yourself. You know I ain't gonna tolerate that shit you spittin', so act right"—Carla paused—"now, as I was saying, I'm calling to check on you. I just wanted to see how your classes were going, if you need anything besides the money I put in your account, you know," Carla said in a motherly tone.

"I'm fine. Damn, when are you gonna stop with all the questions and shit? I mean, I'm in college now and don't like when my *older* sister wants to get in all my business. Listen, Carla, this is my time to find myself, see what I want for my life, have sexual experiences, basically doing shit I want to do—not what you prefer me to do," Serenity spoke with an attitude.

"Damn, I didn't know it was like that." Carla didn't reveal all that she already knew. "All right, if it's like that then I guess you won't be coming out here for your holiday break. Or will you be staying with Rock's peoples?"

"You know what?" Serenity paused. "Carla, you right, I won't be coming home on break or any time soon, for that matter. And for your information, I won't be with Rock's peoples," Serenity replied in a harsh and spiteful voice.

"Oh, now I know what's up. If you mad at that bitch-ass nigga, you better be fuckin' mad at him. Don't fuckin' take that shit out on me. I ain't that bitch-ass nigga." Carla's voice was now irritated and pissed.

"Listen, I gotta go. I gotta do something." Serenity didn't want to just hang up on Carla, so she lied.

"Yeah, no doubt. I'll let you go, Serenity. But before you go I just wanted you to know that I'll be around there in a few days and I would like to stop by or maybe we can do some shopping out there since you ain't coming here for break. I'll call you when I'm there. Cool?" Carla didn't want to be at war with her sister or push her, so she gave her some space to keep things leveled between them.

"Yeah, I'm cool with that. Call me then. Bye." Serenity pressed the END button on her cell phone, not wanting to get even more upset with her sister.

Sadie soon pulled into her driveway after dropping Serenity off at her dorm. She was horny because of the unfinished business that she'd begun just moments before.

"Hope Tootsie's in here," she said to herself getting out the car, then heading to the front door. When she walked in and saw Tootsie sitting at the table working on her laptop, she smiled. She needed to fill a void.

"Hey, baby," Tootsie said standing up and jumping onto Sadie, greeting her with a big, sloppy kiss. "Where have you been? I've been waiting for you. I prepared the rose petal bath and everything," she said in a whining tone.

"Thanks, baby girl. But, I need something else," Sadie said. She popped in a lesbian porno flick. The sounds of the women turned her on. Then she stripped to her boxers and sports bra. She looked at Tootsie while twisting her own nipples. "I wanna taste you. I wanna fuck you. Come fuck your daddy, baby."

Tootsie was irritated that Sadie went out on a one-on-one date with Serenity but didn't let it show. Sadie usually included her when she dealt with other females, especially sexually. It was always the two of them, but with Serenity, Sadie took a different route. Tootsie didn't like what was happening. But without saying a word, she slid out of her gown and prepared to participate in whatever Sadie wanted. She would do anything to keep her attention.

The phone rang loudly.

Oh, boy, here we go . . . let's get it over and done with, Serenity thought, answering her cell phone. "Hey, baby . . . What's up?"

"Oh, you finally fuckin' answer your phone, huh? What's up, Serenity? Why you ain't answering your phone?" Rock barked at her.

"Damn, Rock, you know something I don't? 'Cause the last time I checked, I was grown." Serenity tried not to be irritated.

"Yeah, but you been acting funny. First of all, I haven't seen you in about a week, and we go to the same fuckin' school. Why, Serenity?" Rock asked, agitated.

"Rock, come on, you know I've been busy. You know I'm trying to keep my GPA up and getting into as many student activities as I can. Stop the drama, okay? I'm not doing anything. I should be asking *you* what's up." Serenity hated to lie to him. She put her head down, knowing the first sign of a cheater is they always flip the question back.

“A’ight, fine. Am I gonna see you tonight or what? Can you fit me into your fuckin’ schedule?” Rock asked, still irritated by her unsubstantial answers.

“Yes, I’d love to, but can you save the drama, ’cuz I can’t deal with that shit,” Serenity said, squinting her eyes, knowing he could just hang up and show up at her dorm any minute.

“Yeah, a’ight. I’ll call you. Pick up your phone next time.” Rock’s voice was stern. He hung up the phone knowing something was definitely up with her. *Did I do the right thing? Or have I just fucked up a good thing for my own selfish reasons* he questioned himself.

Damn, I wonder if he knows about what happened at the party. Shit, how the fuck am I gonna explain myself after I dismissed his request over a hundred times? Serenity thought after hanging up the phone. *I guess I’m gonna have to face it, one way or another.*

“Raya, can you come and zip up this damn dress for me?” Serenity said while she stood in front of the mirror and struggled to reach the zipper. She was dressed to impress and was excited about seeing Rock again. Her black tube dress and six-inch stiletto heels had her on point, and she was surely going to be the center of attention wherever they went. Her hair was hanging down to her shoulders, bone straight. As soon as she added her accessories, she would be perfect. Serenity felt guilty and wanted to make it up to him.

“You need some help, ma?” Raya asked.

It was weird hearing Raya call her “ma.” Serenity was

used to niggas calling her that when they wanted to get at her. The fact that it was coming from a woman's mouth felt odd. Goose bumps dotted her neck as awkwardness filled the room.

Raya stared at Serenity through the reflection of the mirror. "You're lucky," she stated.

Raya was standing so close that her lips lightly touched Serenity's neck. The hairs back there stood up.

"Lucky?"

"You look so good tonight. I wish I had your shape," Raya said looking at Serenity's perfectly round ass. She reached for her roommate's necklace on the dresser.

Serenity lifted her hair as Raya placed her necklace on. Then she leaned over and applied one more coat of gloss to her lips. Her dress was so short that she felt a cool draft of air between her legs near her crotch.

Raya ran her fingertip up along Serenity's back.

Serenity tensed up immediately. She was frozen in place. She didn't want to see. She closed her eyes. At first, her breasts were being touched, then kisses were planted at the back of her neck. Suddenly, all of her nerve endings were tingling. Her body was on fire, burning with lust-driven thoughts. Her mind was telling her to just say no, and she formed her lips to utter the words, but Raya's hands were so soft. Her touch was enticing and gentle. Raya was slowly inching Serenity's dress up. Now her entire lower half was bare with the exception of a black lace thong and her stiletto pumps.

"Stop . . . I'm not gay, Raya," she barely whispered.

"Shh . . . I know, ma. I know," she replied. Raya's full

lips pressed against Serenity's and she pulled her thong aside with ease. Raya's fingers explored Serenity intimately, and she felt her wetness. Serenity's tiny thong was soaked, and her sweet cunt smell perfumed the air.

No one will know, Serenity thought. "No one will know," she whispered.

"I won't tell anyone, ma. I just want to make you feel good. Your pussy smells sooo good, Serenity," Raya said softly. Her voice expressed her yearning. It was like she was an addict and Serenity's pussy was the drug of choice.

Serenity's nipples were so erect that they ached and were begging to be sucked. The dark circles of her breasts were now twin pointed missiles, standing sensitive and eager for action. She gasped as she began to grind on Raya's fingers.

"See, Serenity . . . I can make you feel *good*," Raya promised, staring into Serenity's eyes. Serenity was so horny.

Raya loved having straight women. There was something about them that made her nut even better. She was femme all the way and carried herself strictly as a lady. Many niggas tried to get at her and wife her, but she loved pussy. She became an expert at satisfaction by practicing. She often explored her own body, and learned what she liked and disliked. Now she was showing no mercy as she devoured Serenity.

Serenity's clit was throbbing, aching.

Raya eased Serenity onto her bed. Her ass cheeks were hanging out of her dress, leaving her vagina completely exposed. Raya stepped out of her clothes. Her clit was hard and swollen to its maximum potential. She lay on top of Serenity and pressed her body against hers. They were the same height which allowed their bodies to mesh perfectly into each other. Then she starting grinding her clitoris against Serenity's.

Serenity cried out in pleasure. "Yes!" she screamed, gyrating against Raya. "Uh . . . Oh my God!" The feeling was so powerful. It felt better than the sex she ever had with Rock.

They were so wet that they slid effortlessly against one another. The friction and pressure on her clit was almost painful, but it made her feel horny, aggressive, and dominant all at the same time. Serenity licked her lips and watched Raya's breasts bounce up and down. She grabbed one . . . nervously at first, and then put it into her mouth and worked her tongue like a pro.

"Oh, shit," Raya whispered. She wasn't surprised to see that Sadie had opened her up.

The scent of sex was heavy in the air. "Let me taste your pussy," Raya instructed.

At this point, Serenity no longer denied what she truly was. She just wanted Raya to keep going. She sucked on Raya's breasts roughly, biting them a little. She tried to hold back her orgasm because she didn't want it to end.

Raya's lips and tongue finally became acquainted with Serenity's love box.

Serenity pumped her hips and held Raya's head in place to hit that spot immediately. There had never been a feeling so good . . . that she was so sure of. Her cell phone began to ring, but there was no stopping now. They were too engrossed in each other. Serenity now fully understood why her sister had chosen to go both ways, more so one way than the other.

"How does it taste?" Serenity asked, curiously.

"Like sweet honey. You want some?" Raya teased, licking her lips.

She nodded. All of a sudden her tongue was extra wet. She wanted to taste Raya. She knew how it was to get her pussy eaten, but she was curious to know what pussy tasted like.

Raya rolled over onto her back and opened her legs wide, inviting Serenity in.

Serenity stared at her wet, neatly waxed pussy. She was hesitant to go down on her. She had never done it before and didn't want to look like a fool.

Raya noticed it. "Turn around. Let's get into the sixty-nine," she said, hoping Serenity wasn't going to back out.

Serenity's ass was now firmly in Raya's hands, who was pulling her closer to her face. She quickly teased Serenity's clit.

The phone rang again. "Oh, shit, my phone . . . that's probably Rock. Fuck! Damn, I can't do this." Reluctantly, she got out of the position and reached for her phone.

Raya allowed her to get up to answer her phone.

"Baby, what's up? I been calling you. I'm outside waiting," he said.

Raya quickly grabbed Serenity's ass and lifted one of Serenity's legs. She licked her clit vigorously with her tongue and fingered her asshole simultaneously.

"Yeah . . . yeah . . . I was . . . in the . . . mmm," Serenity said, trying to hold back Raya's forceful tongue. "Am coming down now . . . okay . . . baby—" She quickly pressed the END button. "Oh, yeah . . . right *there*," she moaned and grinded against Raya's face. "Oh, I'm cumming!" she screamed. The muscles inside of her contracted, and she felt herself squirt as Raya's mouth invited her release. Serenity was exhausted. She almost fell to the floor trying to move. Her legs were quivering, and her pussy was still throbbing. She was embarrassed as hell and immediately began to feel self-conscious. "What did I just do?" she thought out loud.

"You don't have to be gay to like for a woman to lick your pussy. Just chalk it up to a nice orgasm. Nothing more, nothing less," Raya replied. "Let me know if you ever want to do it again."

"Raya, at this point, I don't know anything. Please, let's keep this between us," she said in a hushed tone. Her face was red from shame, and she was more confused than anything else. She felt embarrassed and dirty, yet her panties and pussy were still creaming at the thought of what had just gone down. She had masturbated plenty of times to thoughts of another woman's touch. But to actually experience it again with a different woman felt like she could do it again . . . and again.

"Don't worry about it," Raya smiled.

Serenity shook her head. She didn't know what she wanted at that moment. It was too awkward, and she knew Raya liked it a little too much. "I'm going to get cleaned up. I'll see you later." She made a mental note to request a new roommate. *I can't have her thinking we're going to be doing this on the regular.*

Raya smiled. "There's nothing to feel bad about, Serenity. You liked it. It's not a big deal. It's between me and you, okay?"

Serenity nodded and gave a half smile, but her mind was still spinning. She couldn't believe another woman made her feel like that. She didn't mean to let it happen. *I wonder what would she say to a threesome with Sadie.*

She sent Rock a text, lying. CHANGING CLOTHES. BE DOWN IN 5. SORRY. She showered quickly, reapplied her makeup, and slipped back into her dress before rushing outside to meet Rock.

They went to dinner and the movies. She noticed that he was acting different. He was very short with her at dinner when answering questions and remained quiet for most of the evening. Finally, she decided to ask him what the fuck his problem was on the ride back.

"Rock, what's the problem? You've had a fuckin' attitude all night long," she said, rubbing the back of his neck. His eyes focused on the road.

"I'm good. Just got a lot on my mind right now," he answered irritated. He shrugged his shoulders in annoyance at her touch.

"Now come on, Rock. I know you better than anyone,

and I know when something is up with you. Is there something you need to tell me?" she said in a stern voice.

Rock was battling his own emotions and didn't know how to approach the situation. He had heard it through the grapevine that she had messed with Sadie in a sexual way. He got the information from a female friend who was a lesbian. Word on campus was "the fine-ass freshman was bi." He didn't know how to feel: jealous or happy. He always had been begging her for a ménage à trois with another woman, but he never thought she would have one without him. Rock pulled his car onto the shoulder of the highway so he could talk to her while looking in her eyes. He couldn't hold it in any longer.

"I heard some shit about you, Serenity," Rock admitted, turning to face her.

Serenity's heart began to speed up as she thought about what she had done lately. *What the fuck? Does he know about Sadie and Tootsie. Did he come to my door and hear me and Raya?* So many things ran through her mind within that brief moment. Her hands began to sweat and a feeling of shame came over her. She dropped her head.

Rock placed his finger under her chin and slightly lifted her head. He had to look into her eyes. "You can tell me anything, baby," he said just before he leaned over and gave her an intimate kiss. He began to get hard as he imagined stroking her from the back while she ate out another female. The plan may have worked after all.

Serenity took a deep breath and decided to come clean, hoping he would not get upset with her. "I went to that big party . . ." she paused and inhaled deeply before breaking the news to him. "And I started to have a lot of drinks while inside. And before I knew it, it was after midnight and that's when everything went down. I let a girl eat me out, but it wasn't nothing to me, I promise. I love only you, Rock. I was dumb, and I let the liquor and my curiosity get the best of me," she said anxiously looking at him, wondering what he was thinking. *Is he mad?* She placed her hand on his thigh.

Rock remained silent. He didn't want to believe what she had just told him. He knew he wanted it to happen. He just didn't want it to be like this. He didn't want the drama. He wanted it to go smooth, an easy transition—with him in the middle. *Well, now that I feel that I am the one who steered her to it, I better get what I want*, he thought. Serenity waited, not knowing what to say next, but she eased up when she saw him crack a smile.

"Did it feel good?" Rock asked, plotting his own hidden agenda for her newfound sexual experience.

Serenity smiled back and nodded at her guilty pleasure. "I can't lie to you. It wasn't as bad as I thought it would be," she admitted evasively.

His manhood began to grow harder. Just the thought had him ready to dive into something wet. "So . . . are you thinking what I'm thinking?" he asked with a devilish grin.

"I think so," she answered shyly. She began to rub him through his pants, making his manhood solid. She knew what he was thinking about, which was a threesome, and it never sounded better to her than it did at that moment. But until then, she wanted to give him a li'l something for taking the news so well. She partially climbed over the seat and pulled out his pole. Then she took him into her mouth and went up and down while twirling her tongue around it. Next, she grabbed his sack and massaged it gently while taking all of him in her mouth.

Rock let his seat back and enjoyed the award-winning head she was putting on him. Superhead could not hold a candle to her on any given night. Serenity's mouth was so warm and so wet. He had taught her well on how to please him.

Serenity wasn't shy about moaning and squirming, giving him more visual and auditory pleasure. Through the years, she worked up to earning her Ph.D. in this special area. This is what you called a *super*blow.

Rock pumped her mouth and held the back of her head. "Oh, here I cum," he moaned, getting even more turned on as he watched his dick disappear deep in her throat. Finally, he exploded. He was the king of the world in his eyes. No one could tell him he couldn't have it all. This was only the prelude of what was to come.

Chapter Seven

Two Weeks Later

The musty smell of sex in the air filled Rock's room as the moonlight shone through the bedroom window. He stroked Serenity from behind while she ate Raya's pussy. He loved the sight and was glad to be a part of what was going down.

Serenity finally agreed to the threesome. She just didn't know Rock had done this all before. He wasn't new to it.

Rock couldn't be happier. And little did he know Serenity had been a part of many threesomes since being turned out by Sadie. But this night was the first time he had a ménage à trois with her. He thought his distance had convinced Serenity to give in. But that wasn't the case at all. She wanted one just as badly as he ever since she got her first taste.

"You like that, huh?" Rock said, watching Serenity's

plump ass bounce back and forth on his crotch. He rubbed her other hole as he plunged in and out of her.

"Yes, daddy," Serenity crooned. She played with Raya's love button as his thrusts became harder and deeper.

Raya rotated her hips and opened her legs wider as Serenity brought her to new heights.

Serenity's words made Rock become stiffer as she began to feel an orgasm about to explode. His pumps became faster and harder as she approached her climax. He grabbed her hips and slammed her ass against his manhood, hearing her moan like never before.

Serenity was in heaven, but her mind wandered. *Okay, usually he's out of the race by now. But yet, he's still got a fucking hard-on. We might have to do this shit more often if this is the result of a fuckin' threesome! Damn!*

After about an hour of straight fucking the shit out of Serenity, he finally pumped one last stroke before exploding inside her ass. Finished, he slid out of her and walked into the bathroom. He expected to hear her footsteps behind him, but instead, he heard loud moans. After peeing and washing his dick off, he quickly entered the room. He was completely exhausted. He thought that would be the end of the threesome, but it was only the beginning for Serenity and Raya. He watched Serenity in a sixty-nine position. He frowned, looking confused, noticing that she looked way too comfortable; almost natural.

"Damn, baby, can I get in?" he interrupted, inching closer to the bed. Standing there, he got a better angle to watch Serenity flick her tongue swiftly against Raya's clit. His words fell on deaf ears, and neither of the women responded. *Are you serious?* he thought.

Actually, they both had forgotten he was even there. Sadie had completely turned Serenity out, and Raya loved every minute of it.

After watching for close to half an hour, Rock grew disappointed and slightly jealous. Raya had brought Serenity to an orgasm at least five times before he had a chance to do it twice. *Damn, she never shook like that when she bustin' a nut with me*, he thought, putting on his boxers with a major attitude.

Without saying a word, Raya slipped to the bathroom and then left. But just before she exited the room, she tongue-kissed Serenity while she looked into Rock's eyes. He grew furious but remained silent.

Serenity was smiling and breathing hard. She rolled over on the bed. "That was great, baby. Are you happy now?" she asked.

"The real question is, are *you* happy now? You seemed to be enjoying yourself a little too much," he said looking at her.

"What the fuck is *that* supposed to mean?" She sat up quickly and looked at him directly in his face.

"You know what the fuck I'm talking about. First, you denied me totally. But then you go to this party and have some next bitch eat your pussy—my pussy. You ain't even let me know you were feeling that way. What the fuck, Serenity?" Rock said, getting more heated.

"Hold up! You the one who wanted a threesome. I

was just trying to please you and make our sex life better. Don't get to acting all stupid all of a sudden, Rock. You asked for this, not me," she said, snatching her panties off the bed and shaking her head in total disbelief. "I can't believe this motherfucka," she whispered to herself loud enough for him to hear her.

"I saw how you were eating her pussy! You weren't exactly an amateur at that shit. You fucked her before? Huh? You gonna let Sadie turn you out, too? Huh? Like she do all these stupid bitches on campus?" he yelled.

"I haven't done anything with her before, Rock. You know that. What you mean Sadie gonna turn me out?" she asked, contemplating on what he knew.

"Yeah, okay. If that's how you get down, then a'ight," Rock huffed.

"You know what? Fuck you, nigga. I try to satisfy you, and you get mad at me? What, are you *jealous* because she knew how to eat my pussy *better* than you?" Serenity snapped and stepped closer to Rock.

"Bitch, fuck you! You said that was my pussy, but from what I saw, you done tripped and landed yourself in some shit!" Rock yelled as spit flew out of his mouth.

Serenity's few words had just crushed his ego.

"Bitch? I got your bitch. This ain't yours, nigga, it's mine. You don't own me. I can fuck, suck, lick whoever the fuck I want," Serenity retorted, stunned by his words.

Rock had never called her out of her name until then.

"You know what, Rock? Fuck you!" Serenity said just

before storming out of his room and exiting his apartment.

Rock didn't know it, but he was pushing Serenity away from him and straight into Sadie's arms.

Serenity cried in Sadie's arms, telling her about how Rock had flipped out on her.

Sadie held her, comforting her while her girl squad was sitting around them. She told Serenity everything she wanted to hear. She knew this was her opportunity to slide right on in. As she stroked Serenity's hair, loud banging noises came from her front door.

"Go get that!" Sadie yelled at one girl. She was furious at the disrespect shown to her by the person who was banging on the door like they were the police. Moments later, she heard her girl yelling.

"You can't come in here! Get the fuck out!"

Everyone's attention was focused at the front of the house where the yelling was coming. The shouts became closer. That's when Rock appeared.

"I knew yo' ass was gonna come here. Come on! Let's go!" Rock shouted, grabbing Serenity's arm and pulling her up.

Sadie played it cool and smiled when Serenity was ripped from her embrace.

"You better hold your horses, my man. You running up in the wrong spot with that shit," Sadie said standing up and rubbing her chin with her fingers, without an ounce of fear in her heart.

"What the fuck you mean? You better step the fuck off, you dyke bitch! I know what you about," Rock barked at her.

"I think you better leave. Serenity is staying here, playboy," Sadie said reaching her hand out.

On cue, two of the girls behind Rock pulled out 9 mm pistols and pointed them at him, leaving him shaken.

Rock's eyes widened. He stood absolutely still, knowing if he made a move, the outcome would be painful.

"What's that? I can't hear you. You don't seem to have a lot to say anymore, huh? Like I said, I think it's time for you to leave, my man. You smell me now, nigga?" Sadie smirked.

Serenity stepped toward Sadie and grabbed her hand. "Leave, Rock," she said, leaning on Sadie and staring into his eyes.

Rock stared back at Serenity. He didn't want to show any emotion. He wanted Sadie to know there was no love lost. He turned around and walked toward the front door and left, not saying a word. He was emotionally floored. He wanted to hurt Sadie in every way possible. His love had just been snatched by a woman. His pride was crushed. He walked away, shaking his head in disbelief. His heart was broken. Even though he fucked around on Serenity, he really did love her, and he was devastated.

He got to his car and sat in it. Then he pulled his cell phone out and dialed. "Yo', she left me. What the fuck did you exactly do? We gotta talk *now*."

Chapter Eight

It was the night of the men's conference finals and also the last home game for the team. The place was packed, and Rock sat with a couple of his football teammates in the stands waiting for the game to start. He wanted to have a good time, but he found himself thinking about Serenity constantly. He hadn't spoken to her in two weeks, and she wasn't taking any of his calls. *I really miss that girl*, he thought, hoping to see her at the game. Just as he scanned the auditorium, he saw Raya, her roommate.

"Yo', I'll be right back," Rock said to his friends and stood up. He headed toward Raya. He shuffled through the crowd and made his way to her. She was standing against the wall watching the crowd from the near entrance.

"Yo', what up?" Rock greeted her with a smile.

"Hey, what up? What's crackin'?" Raya smiled and held out her hand.

"You seen Serenity? I've been calling her, and I stopped by a few times and got no answer," Rock said, trying to be as nonchalant as possible. He didn't want to seem like he was stalking her. He didn't want to admit that he missed her to anybody but himself.

"Actually, I haven't been seeing a lot of her lately. She hasn't even been staying in the room at night for the past couple of weeks," Raya said, not knowing she was breaking Rock's heart with every word.

"Oh, for real?" he asked coolly, boiling on the inside. He then noticed that everyone's attention shifted to the side entrance, where a group of women entered, and among them was Serenity. She was right under the arm of Sadie. He couldn't believe what he was seeing. His face instantly frowned as he watched his ex being escorted by a female.

Sadie was famous for having the most beautiful women in her entourage, and from the looks of it, she just recruited a top-notch freshman named Serenity. It was official. She was her chick.

After just the first night at Sadie's, Serenity was hooked. She snorted as much cocaine as she wanted and was pleased sexually every step of the way. She embraced all the attention she received.

"Speaking of the devil," Raya said to Rock pointing at the gathering crowd.

"Ain't that 'bout a bitch?" he said under his breath, and he stormed over toward the crowd.

Sadie was whispering in Serenity's ear, and she was giggling like a little girl, obviously loving whatever Sadie was telling her.

"Serenity, we need to talk," Rock said with folded arms, standing in front of them, blocking their view of the court.

"Oh, shit, look who we have here. Stone . . . No, I mean Rocky. What's your name again?" Sadie asked with a smug grin on her face, making her whole crew laugh.

Rock kept his eyes on Serenity and hoped that she would just talk to him. She never looked his way.

"Serenity, just talk to me. You know this is not you," Rock pleaded, trying to make eye contact.

Sadie continued to whisper in Serenity's ear, making her giggle some more.

When Rock finally got a glance at Serenity's pupils, he realized that she was high off of something, and it crushed him. He felt his heart beating in slow motion.

"It looks like she doesn't have any words for you, Rocky. So, I would like for you to bounce before I get upset," Sadie said looking past Rock and seeing her brother at the opposite side of the court sitting with his crew.

Rock followed her eyes and saw Shawn P and his crew mugging him. He turned to Serenity one last time. "Serenity, you can always come back. I'm so sorry for calling you out of your name. I just want you to know that I love you and would never intentionally hurt you," he said, laying all his cards out, hoping she would give him some sign.

Serenity ignored him.

The way her body was swaying back and forth, it was obvious that she was as high as a kite. Sadie had given her a couple of lines to hit just before they came into the building. She was zooted.

Rock walked away and knew that once a good girl goes bad, she's gone forever. He had lost her. He would have to get up with Shawn P later to find out why his crew was peeping him so hard.

"Yo', why he steppin' to like that? Watch him; it looks like my sister done pissed off another nigga," Shawn P said, staring at Rock. "Hell, yeah, she done fucked with this nigga's pussy. Damn, I told her about that shit."

"Yo', P, that nigga is suppose to handle that deal from Cali, remember?" one of Shawn P's boys said.

"Oh, fuck. Well, find out why the fuck he steppin' to my sister like he wanna start some shit," Shawn P ordered. His boy immediately went to work to get the lowdown on what was happening.

Shawn P knew Rock from his service of getting drugs moved throughout the state. At that time, the city was still on lock with all the 9/11 shit going on.

Rock started hustling when the scouts used to bring him to the schools to entice him. He had hooked up with this one chick named Iris. She was his connection to the main players in the game. She would set up the pickup and drop-off location. He brought drugs from point A to point B. When the drugs got to their destination, Iris would be there to collect the payment.

Rock became well-known for moving a lot of dope at one time. After accepting his full athletic scholarship to college, he developed a chronic service. He knew he could still continue with shifting dope around, but he wanted to keep it to a more controlled environment. He used his popularity to get all his clientele. It was a slow bubble but steady money. After six months of promoting and tweaking his system, he made close to ten Gs every two weeks.

Shawn P sent a text to his sister. WHAT THE FUCK IS GOIN' DOWN?

YOUR MAN WANTS HER BACK. LOL. Sadie replied back.

YO, MEET ME ON THE OUTSIDE IN 5, Shawn P texted quickly

SURE, Sadie replied.

Sadie stood up to go meet her brother and find out why was he so bothered.

"Yo', what the fuck is going on between you and that nigga?" Shawn P cut straight to the point.

"What the fuck you all upset about? That nigga ain't nobody to you," Sadie retorted back.

"Look, that nigga is supposed to do me a favor with some shit. Some money shit, so I don't want you to fuck up my shit, you hear? So put that bullshit on a fucking halt for now. Didn't I tell you about fucking with these campus bitches? Their niggas don't like when a bitch thinks she got bigger balls than them," Shawn P said with frustration in his voice.

"Shawn, that motherfucka done straight-up lost his chick . . . I mean, it ain't my fault she digging me and don't want his ass no more. Beside, if that nigga is true to his game, all this here"—Sadie stepped back—"don't got nothing to do with your shit with him. Are we good?" Sadie said with her eyes locked on his.

Shawn P sucked his teeth, then flashed a grin. "Yeah, yeah, we good, sis. This would be the test of a true hustler. But you know what pussy can do. Don't make the wrong decision, 'cause I ain't stopping no nigga from beatin' your ass down if my money gets fucked up 'cause of some soap-opera bullshit," Shawn P said laughing. "Man, I'm going back to the game. I just wanted you to know what was up."

"A'ight, P, don't stress. See ya around," Sadie said smiling and walking back to her seat.

Serenity smiled feeling the kisses from Sadie waking her up. The sun's beams shined through the bedroom windows and the rays warmed her skin, proclaiming morning.

"Good morning, baby," Sadie whispered, cupping one of Serenity's breasts.

"Good morning," Serenity said, rubbing her eyes.

Sadie pecked her on the lips and walked into the bathroom naked, showing off her tattooed back: a collage of guns.

Serenity admired her body. Sadie's plump ass and toned legs would have been any man's dream, but she would never have that. She had never been with a man and had no desire to.

Once the water started running for the shower, Serenity took the opportunity to examine the bedroom, admiring the immaculate, spacious room. The wooden floors and fireplace made the room look warm and cozy. It was obvious that Sadie had spent a lot of money on it, and she was definitely impressed. Serenity climbed out of bed and took off her panties, then walked to the bathroom to join Sadie.

The bathroom was steamy, and Sadie didn't notice her walking in. She only noticed when the shower door opened.

Serenity stepped into the shower. The two women began to kiss while the hot water cascaded down both of their bodies. They rubbed each other and pressed their nipples against one another, both of them becoming quickly aroused. Next, Sadie dropped to her knees and Serenity propped her leg up on the soap dish for easy access. Sadie grabbed both of Serenity's butt cheeks and sucked away at her love box with no inhibitions. Serenity moaned and thrust her pelvis against Sadie's face, harder and harder with each thrust. Sadie then took two fingers and inserted them into Serenity slowly and gently while her tongue flicked hungrily on her button.

"Sadie, you are the best," Serenity moaned, gripping the back of her head and letting the hot water hit her face and flow down her body.

Finally, Sadie stood up and led Serenity back to the bedroom, still dripping wet from the shower.

"Lie down," she ordered.

Serenity did as she was told, eagerly waiting to see what Sadie had in store for her.

Sadie walked over to her dresser and pulled out her strap-on. She put it on and then rubbed the rubber dildo that hung in front of her. She groped it like her own. Then she grabbed a rabbit and turned the switch on.

The buzzing sound filled the room, and Serenity separated her legs, knowing the anticipation was driving her crazy.

Sadie climbed on top of Serenity and placed the rabbit directly on her clit, causing her to flinch. She then entered her wound and began to slowly pump.

Serenity watched Sadie's ass rotate in the mirror on the closet facing the bed. She loved the way Sadie was stroking her. It was unlike any feeling she ever had. She worked her strap as if she were born with it. Sadie was a master at her sex craft.

"Oh . . . oh, that feels sooo good," Serenity moaned, grabbing Sadie's ass and moving to her rhythmic motions.

Now Sadie tossed the rabbit to the side and went

deeper into Serenity's flesh and sucked on her neck gently.

By now, Serenity was soaking wet, and her juices were creating a small puddle on the bed. Noises from Sadie slamming her hard strap-on into Serenity's hot, wet pussy echoed through the house.

Sadie put it on her like she would never forget it.

Next, Sadie flipped her over and then entered her from behind. She licked her thumb and tenderly placed it over Serenity's other hole, massaging it and stroking her pussy deeply. She was putting work in and turning Serenity into a certified freak—just the way she liked her women. She loved the way Serenity's ass jiggled every time she plunged into her. She could feel the pressure on her clit every time she pumped her. Unlike any guy, Sadie could reach an orgasm and keep going. She knew by Serenity's body movements that she was approaching an orgasm, so she sped up and slammed her strokes harder.

"You like that?" Sadie asked, slapping Serenity's ass cheeks.

"Yes! Yes, Sadie!" Serenity yelled, clutching the sheets, nearly yanking them off the bed. "Oh, God. I'm about to cum . . ." Serenity screamed.

"Cum on this dick, baby," Sadie screamed, slipping her thumb deep into Serenity's asshole.

"I love this dick. Oh, fuck . . ." Serenity yelled out. Her legs quivered as she lay flat on her stomach totally satisfied.

At that moment, Sadie knew that she owned Serenity's mind and body. She smiled and slid out of her and went to work with her tongue.

Tootsie stood behind the door with tears building in her eyes. She heard every moan.

Sadie glanced at the cracked door and saw Tootsie's shadow. She was the only woman allowed to have a key to her house before Serenity showed up. She pondered how she was going to fix things with Tootsie. She had to fix it.

Chapter Nine

Serenity was unofficially Sadie's love. The more time she spent with Sadie, the more she felt for her. However, the closer they got, the farther Tootsie faded out of the picture. Their hot, steamy ménage à trois no longer was a nightly ritual. It became more of a scene straight out of some corny romance movie.

Tootsie acted more as the server than the once adored, never-want-for-anything main chick of Sadie's. She felt like the third wheel. She sat on Sadie's throne-like chair with a clear view to the backyard pool. "I hate that bitch," she murmured to herself watching them splash water on each other. Angry, she took the school ID that sat on the table and lined up some coke before her.

Sadie had an endless supply from her brother Shawn P, and she took advantage of it. She liked to keep it around for her parties and to make some quick cash.

Tootsie had been getting high more frequently than usual, trying to cope with her changing relationship with Sadie. She lowered her head closer to the table, and her nostrils devoured the lines. Then she quickly threw her head back, sat back in the chair, and closed her eyes, waiting for the drug to administer its magic. She felt unwelcomed. She couldn't deal with Serenity moving into her spot so smoothly.

Sadie and Serenity laughed, playing childishly. Sadie wore loose swimming trunks and a sports bra, while Serenity had on a sexy two piece, leaving nothing to the imagination. She sat on the edge of the pool, with Sadie in the water between her legs.

"Serenity, I want you to be mine . . . for better or for worse," Sadie said looking up at her.

Serenity, with a sober mind, felt the realness in every word she said. Her stomach felt like it had butterflies in it. She never meant to lead Sadie on or even have a relationship.

She loved the way Sadie made her feel, or at least that's what she wanted to believe. She thought back to the time they were together. She remembered half the time they were getting high off of blow, partying, smoking weed, and having unpredictable orgies. She didn't know how to respond to Sadie's comment because although she and Rock weren't speaking, she still loved him. She took her time before speaking to make sure her mind and words were clear.

"Sadie, I don't know how to say this, but I just don't feel the same. These past months were like a fog of fantasies. I don't want to hurt you. I'm not the woman who wants you. Rock is the only person I will truly love. As much as I loved being with you, a woman, I must admit I was just curious." She spoke in her most sincere voice, draping her arms around Sadie, gently kissing her on the lips. "I should go get my things and leave. I'm sorry, Sadie. I didn't expect this to happen." She tried to stand, but Sadie's grip on her thighs made it impossible.

"But Serenity—" Sadie responded with tears building in her eyes and her grip tightening.

"Sadie, I think it's best," Serenity cut her short. "Our relationship was based solely on sex. Great sex, I should add. But you just can't have me. I'm just not ready to commit to you. Now, let me go!"

Sadie reluctantly released her grip.

Serenity quickly stood up and walked into the house.

Sadie's ego took a huge blow with Serenity's words. She had never experienced rejection before, and it was her first time actually hearing "no." But she played it cool and smiled. She watched Serenity's ass cheeks jiggle as she walked off and vowed it wasn't going to be the last time. *What Sadie wants, Sadie gets!* She began to put a plan together. Her blood was boiling, and she was determined to make Serenity hers, no matter what. For the first time, she felt like she was in love. She knew if Rock had been out of the picture for good Serenity would be hers.

Serenity left Sadie standing in the pool looking like she lost her puppy. She saw Tootsie in Sadie's chair with her buzz on and didn't say a word. She went into the bedroom and packed whatever she could fit into her oversized night bag and walked to the front door where she was stopped.

"Oh, so you leaving now? So that's it. You got your rocks off and made her want you like no one else. You think you can just leave her. She ain't gonna let you go. You better not come back, bitch. You done created a whole lot of pain that I'm gonna be dealing with. You should of never came to that party. You should of stayed in your motherfuckin' place and knew who her main chick was," Tootsie spat out with hatred.

"Look, Tootsie, it's over between her and me. So go comfort your fuckin' *daddy*, you dumb fuckin' ho." Serenity pushed her out of the way and walked out the door.

The crisp night air gave Serenity a renewed sense. Her mind was clear about who she was and what she wanted. Her haze was lifted. She reached for her phone out of the side pocket of her night bag.

Baby, please pick up. Serenity's only thought was she needed to talk to Rock. She took a cab to his house immediately.

"You going to do this for me, right, baby girl?" Sadie asked Tootsie while stroking her hair. They were both completely naked in bed and sweating. Sadie had just made Tootsie cum over and over again and put her strap-on to work. She was trying to get back on Tootsie's good side since she had been neglecting her sexually ever since Serenity came into the picture. She also needed Tootsie's cooperation for the plan to be successful.

"So, you want me to kill him?" Tootsie asked with fear in her voice and uncertainty in her heart.

"Yeah, that nigga has to go," Sadie said. She reached over to the nightstand and grabbed a blunt, lit it, and gave it to Tootsie.

Tootsie took a deep hit off it and knew it tasted funny right away. And the smell was different from the usual weed that Sadie had.

This was custom-made, especially for Tootsie. Sadie laced the blunt with coke. She wanted to alter Tootsie's thinking and control her any way she could. Sadie was no longer attracted to Tootsie, but she wouldn't let her know that. She needed her to take care of Rock before she dumped Tootsie for good.

"Why do you want him dead, Sadie?" Tootsie asked out of curiosity.

Sadie knew that it wasn't a good enough reason for him to be killed. But in her eyes, having someone who she loved was a good enough reason, enough to die. "If you do this for me, my heart would be secured with your love, baby girl. No one would ever be able to replace you," Sadie said, watching her take another hit of the laced blunt. "Do you want some nose candy too, baby girl?"

"You . . . You would love me more? I would be locked into your heart, honestly?" Tootsie asked.

"Yeah, I would know that you are down for me, ya know. I wanna make sure you with me no matter what," Sadie lied.

Tootsie's eyes lit up like the sky on the Fourth of July. She was so deeply in love with Sadie she was willing to do anything to secure her love. At the thought of being the only one, she wanted to scream with excitement. She believed the lies. In her mind, Sadie promised that with the killing of Rock, their love would be secure forever.

Serenity looked at her cell phone and saw her sister, Carla, was calling. She quickly sent her to voice mail. Carla was calling her nonstop. She had been avoiding the calls for one reason only: she didn't want to talk about Sadie or what drugs she was on when she hooked up with her. She absolutely knew that her sister heard all about it. Carla had eyes and ears everywhere. Serenity half expected her sister to just catch a plane out here like usual.

Serenity stood at Rock's door with her bag and her phone in hand, sobbing. She looked at her phone and redialed his number. It went straight to voice mail—again. Finally, she wiped her eyes and decided to go to her dorm. Maybe she could settle her head there.

Chapter Ten

Rock and his entourage threw money on the stage while the well-proportioned stripper did tricks up and down the pole. It was just past midnight, and the liquor was flowing, and good times were present. It was the first time he had enjoyed himself in months.

Serenity had been on his mind heavily lately. Tonight, his friends forced him to get out and enjoy himself to get his mind off her. They watched the stripper climb to the top of the pole, then slid down, landing in a full split, making her ass bounce up and down. Her big, bouncy ass and the juicy lips of her pussy left nothing for the imagination even though she wore a skimpy thong. The crowd erupted in applause, standing up. She rotated her hips seductively, making her ass cheeks clap together to the beat of Gyptian's latest hit. Out of nowhere, twenty-dollar bills began to hit the stage and everyone's attention shifted to who was making it rain: Sadie Smith.

She was on the top level throwing down wads and wads of cash, totally taking over the club. Strippers flocked to the stage trying to get a piece of the action, knowing Sadie was a heavy tipper who wasn't shy about making it rain when she was in the house.

Rock instantly got tight, and his mood completely changed looking at the woman who took his girl and was now overshadowing his crew with her money. He scanned around Sadie, hoping to see Serenity, but she was nowhere in sight.

"I have to drain the main vein," Rock said to his friend, finishing his glass of Hennessey and slamming it on the table with force before leaving. He stood up, staggered, and headed to the bathroom. When he approached the back of the club, he saw Tootsie coming out of the women's restroom.

Both of them stopped in their tracks and just for a split second stared at each other. He gave her a dirty look and gruffly brushed past her. She grabbed his arm and turned him toward her. He snatched his arm back and sucked his teeth, growing irritated by her touch.

"Come here, daddy," she said in a seductive voice. She was smiling from ear to ear.

"I don't have a lot to smile about," Rock said between his clenched teeth.

Tootsie could see the building anger in his face. His jaw muscles tightened noticeably.

"Don't be like that," she said stepping closer to him.

He looked at her and saw that she was wearing his favorite color, red. She had on a tight-fitting red dress that hugged her body showing all her curves, with red stilettos, and a red lollipop in her mouth. He didn't want to admit it, but she was looking very attractive. Her nice, firm legs and plump ass made his manhood jump slightly in his pants.

"I know you want it, Rock. I see the way you looking at me," Tootsie said, boldly gazing at his crotch, moving even closer and twirling the lollipop slowly inside of her mouth. She was showing him how well she could work her tongue.

"You're barking up the wrong tree, ma. You know I can't fuck with you like that. Yeah, your bitch made me lose my girl. I don't want anything to do with that dyke bitch," Rock said bitterly, putting his hands up, stopping her from getting any closer.

"What? You talking about Sadie? That bitch. Pleeease. I think I need something new, something I can *really* touch," Tootsie said shifting her weight to one side and putting her hand on her hip. "Sadie is old news, daddy. I don't fuck with her like that no more. She's so far up Serenity's ass that we don't even kick it like that anymore. So what's up with me and you? I can see you ready for me," Tootsie said noticing the bulge in his jeans. She went for it and grabbed his rod and began stroking it while it was still in his jeans.

Rock wanted to slap her hand away, but it felt too good.

"I ain't fucking with you," Rock said, smiling and cupping one of her voluptuous breasts.

"I don't believe you," Tootsie said slowly, pushing him back into the men's room.

He allowed himself to be guided backward into the bathroom.

Tootsie began to kiss him passionately while pushing him directly into a bathroom stall, making him fall down onto the toilet seat. She wasted no time dropping to her knees. She unbuckled his pants, releasing his big rod, and took him into her mouth. She made sure her mouth was extra juicy when she sucked on him. Then she pulled his pants all the way down to his ankles and began to massage his balls. She slurped him up and down like he was her lollipop.

Rock could only smile looking down, watching her make his tool disappear and reappear like magic. It was sweet revenge for him to see one of Sadie's main bitches giving him head and loving it.

Tootsie ran her tongue up and down the base of his pole, hitting all the right spots. Suddenly, she slipped her hands down to her honeypot between her legs and began to rub herself while still pleasing him. She even hummed lightly like a well tuned guitar.

The fact that he was getting pleased in a public place turned him on even more. He saw the veins on his penis swelling from excitement. He lifted his butt off the seat and began to pump her mouth, trying to touch her tonsils. He didn't think her head game would be good, but he learned quickly how wrong he was.

She took all of him in without any trouble, showing no signs of a gag reflex. She felt him clenching his butt cheeks and felt his rod getting even harder, knowing he was about to cum. Abruptly, she took her mouth off him and stood up, stopping his pleasure.

"What's up? Why you stop?" he asked, looking confused and desperate.

"I want to get fucked," Tootsie said, continuing to rub her clit right in front of his face.

"I got you. Get on it," he said, becoming harder and wanting to fuck her even more.

"I want to fuck you good, daddy," she said taking her fingers off her clit and putting them in her mouth, sucking them one by one.

"Man, you playing. You gonna leave your daddy like this?" he asked with his hard dick in hand, slowly jerking it.

"I have a room at the Marriot for the night. If you *really* wanna get it poppin', then let's go. I'm horny as fuck and haven't had a real big cock in me in years," she stated bluntly, grabbing his pole and straddling him. She let the tip of his rod barely touch her pussy lips so that he could feel how wet and ready she was. He tried to enter her, but she quickly jumped back and walked out of the stall. "I'll be waiting by your car outside. Don't have me waiting long, nigga," she said, walking out the bathroom, switching her ass hard.

Rock was totally open and did not even think twice about going with Tootsie to the hotel. He was thinking with his little head rather than the big one up top. "I'm about to fuck the shit outta that bitch. She don't know who she fuckin' with," he said, zipping his pants up and following her out of the bathroom like an obedient puppy. He smiled glancing at Sadie on the way out of the back entrance.

Serenity reached for her cell phone on her desk and dialed Rock's number again. *Have I lost him for good? Why won't he answer my calls?* she wondered, hearing his voice mail message begin. She pressed the END button before the beep sounded. *Damn, I ruined everything with my curiosity!*

Chapter Eleven

Rock entered the hotel room anticipating Tootsie's every move.

She was in the bathroom snorting lines of coke.

He sat on the bed and wished that he could see Sadie's face and make her angry and embarrassed. If she only knew that he was about to fuck the shit out of one of her bitches. He heard the shower turn on and knew Tootsie was about to take a shower before they got it hot and heavy.

"Stanky bitch," Rock said lying back on the bed. He quickly sat up and got an idea that would definitely embarrass Sadie and hopefully make her ass think twice about trying to turn out some next nigga's chick. His camcorder was in his car. The thought of taping Tootsie sucking his dick, fucking him, and calling him *daddy* would positively get Sadie upset. He would load it to every social link he could, YouTube, MySpace, Facebook, anything so that everyone that hangs with her would know her girl ain't all that exclusive. *I don't give a shit about that stanky fuckin' bitch anyway. She probably fucked Serenity too*, he thought, feeling a brief second of guilt about making a recording. But that guilt was short-lived after he thought about his revenge on Sadie and what she did to ruin his relationship with Serenity.

Rock quickly jumped up, grabbed his keys, and eased his way out of the room door, wanting to return before Tootsie got out of the shower. He ran to his car to retrieve his camera from the trunk. Upon entering the room, he still heard the shower running and was happy he thought and moved so quickly.

Rock knew that he only had a matter of minutes before she came out, so he scanned the room quickly to find the best way to hide the camera, voyeur style. He adjusted the camera to point directly to the bed, all while trying to decide how to disguise it. He ended up setting it up near the television and put a hotel towel over the camera to hide it.

Tootsie turned off the shower and stepped out. She grabbed a towel to dry off and snorted a few more lines.

Rock jumped onto the bed, removed his jeans, and tried to act normal.

Moments later, Tootsie came out wrapped in a towel, and then the towel dropped. She was completely naked.

Rock smiled, starting to stroke his dick. His adrenaline began to pump, thinking about being recorded. He was getting off on the idea.

She walked over to him and straddled him, kissing him all over. "Oh, daddy, I want you so badly," she cooed, placing her hand on his while he was jerking his rod and getting hard. Then she slid down to the floor onto her knees.

He remained lying down, staring at the hidden camera.

But little did he know, Tootsie was reaching for a gun and preparing to take his life. She had called Sadie from the bathroom to let her know that the plan was in motion.

Sadie was on the outside of the hotel room door, waiting to hear the gunshot so she could come in and clean off Tootsie's prints and remove any other evidence from the room.

Rock closed his eyes and enjoyed the feeling of Tootsie's touch.

She quickly glanced up at him. He was so into it that he didn't notice when she went for the 9 mm gun hidden under the bed. She reached for the gun while he was still in her mouth.

"Yeah, bitch, who your fucking daddy, huh? You like this *real* dick, right?" he asked, wanting her answer to seal her fate.

"Mmm . . . You my daddy, baby . . . yeah, I love this big, real cock," she replied easily, pulling her mouth away from his dick.

"I'ma bust all over your fuckin' face, bitch . . . mmm . . . shit . . . Yeah, suck this dick," Rock said, not wanting her stop.

She stopped sucking him.

He sat up to see why. What he saw startled him and nearly made him piss and shit himself. He was looking down the barrel of a 9 mm gun.

Her index finger was on the trigger. Her hands were shaking. Before he could let off a word, she shot directly into the middle of his head, making his body jerk back and fall to the bed. He lay still without a sound.

Tootsie stood over him. She dropped the smoking gun and her nerves got the best of her.

Seconds later, Sadie opened the door with the spare key. She smiled, knowing she had one less problem. She knew with him gone, Serenity would cling to her even tighter. A twisted grin plastered Sadie's face. She quickly wiped the room down and the gun.

"You did good, baby. You did good," Sadie said stroking her hair and kissing her on the forehead. She led Tootsie back into the bathroom and into the tub, then she turned the water on and washed Tootsie's body with a washcloth she brought. She was so turned on by the idea of Serenity running back into her arms she began to rub Tootsie's clit, pretending it was Serenity's.

"Yeah, daddy, I did it for you," Tootsie whispered to Sadie.

Sadie grabbed her breast and started to twist her nipple while jamming her three fingers into Tootsie's pussy.

She moved her fingers swiftly in and out to make Tootsie cum on cue.

Sadie knew she didn't have too much time left to clean up. She said, "Baby girl, we gotta get outta here. Put this robe on now and use the bottom of the robe to open the door. Once you're out the door, put your flip-flops on and walk straight down the hall to staircase B. That leads you to the side entrance of the parking lot. There's a black Camry parked out front in the first parking space to your left. The door is unlocked on the driver's side. The keys are in the cup holder, some money and nose candy are in the glove compartment. Go to the Four Seasons and stay there until I call you. Here's the key. I love you, baby girl. I can't wait for us to be together."

As Tootsie stepped out the door, Sadie got to work quickly. It was then that she glanced over at the TV and saw a towel covering something right next to it. She walked over and lifted the towel to discover a small camcorder. "This motherfucka. I could only imagine what he would of done with this shit. Too bad, nigga." Sadie looked over at Rock's slumped corpse and laughed. She noticed the camera was still recording and turned it onto herself. "Shh . . ."

A week went past and Serenity could not believe Rock would do her like that. She thought she would have seen him or heard from him by now. She called him at least a hundred times after she left Sadie but only got his voice mail. She also stopped at his house all different times of the day, but there was no answer. Her heart grew worried.

One day, she heard her cell phone ring and quickly looked at it, hoping it was Rock. She answered, "Hi, Sadie, how are you?"

"Hey, you finally ready to talk to me. I tried calling you ever since you left my house," Sadie said, happy to hear her voice. "Look, I just wanna say that I didn't mean to make you rush into anything you're not sure of. And I definitely didn't mean to provide you with drugs if you weren't ready for it. I'm sorry."

"Thank you. But I won't put all the blame on you. You sure didn't hold a gun to my head," Serenity chuckled.

"Can we start all over again? Can we forget the parties, forget everything and just start over? I really would like to be your friend," Sadie pleaded.

"Forget everything? I can't forget everything. Listen, you made me feel good. I mean, so did the drugs, but I don't want or need that shit. You taught me not to be reserved about wanting a woman. You taught me how much a woman can please me just as any man can. So I won't forget," Serenity said unruffled.

"Well, in that case, come over so we can reenact what we had. Just us, no one else unless you want it that way," Sadie boldly said, hoping her bluntness would work.

Serenity laughed, deciding not to say yes immediately. "I gotta get this paper done, and besides, I got an early class tomorrow."

"What's the paper on?" Sadie asked.

"The influences of music on youth today. You sound like you gonna help me or something."

"I might be able to. You should come over so I can." Sadie hoped she would. "I could come get you."

"Okay, but you better help me on this paper. How long you gonna be?" Serenity asked, wanting someone familiar to hold. She knew she lost Rock. He wasn't returning her calls, nor was he at his house. She figured if he didn't want her, why not go to someone who did.

"I'm actually outside. Come on out," Sadie said.

"Damn, what you doing in front of my dorm?" Serenity asked, putting her laptop in its bag and heading downstairs.

"Umm . . . I was hoping to see you. I mean, you didn't pick up your phone when I called," Sadie said quickly.

"Okay, but how did you know which dorm? You know I'm no longer roommates with Raya. I switched to the other dorm building."

"What? You forgot who I am? I just ask, and I get answers. Now, we done spent at least five minutes on the phone when you could have used those five minutes to come outside and talk to me for real," Sadie said, trying to get Serenity outside and off the phone.

"Uh-huh, I'm through the doors. Open up." Serenity knocked at the car window.

Sadie opened the car door.

Serenity got in and closed her phone. "What? You forgot who I am?"

They both laughed and headed to Sadie's house.

"No!" Serenity screamed, seeing Rock's picture on the news. The reporter described the heinous crime in-depth, and she watched along with Sadie. The reporter stated that his body had been in a hotel room for two days before it was finally discovered by maid service. They had no suspects at this time, and it looked like a drug deal gone bad.

Sadie put her hand over her mouth in sudden shock, but in actuality, she was smiling under her hand. "Oh my God. I'm so sorry," Sadie said, taking Serenity into her arms. "Who would do something like this?" Sadie asked, stroking Serenity's hair and rubbing her back.

"I can't believe this! Why would somebody want to hurt Rock?" Serenity sobbed, standing up and running into the bedroom. She slammed the door behind her. Her heart was broken.

Sadie calmly smiled, watching Serenity race to the bedroom. Then she used her nail to split a Dutch Master and rolled a blunt with D.C.'s finest chronic, courtesy of Rock himself. She sparked the blunt, put her feet on her coffee table, and paused the TV. His face was all over the screen, and she stared at it. *Sadie gets what she wants*, she thought with a big smile from ear to ear. She deeply inhaled.

She looked at her watch and wondered where Tootsie was. She usually called at five o'clock, after her classes. It was now approaching six, and Sadie wanted to talk to her to make sure her head was all right after what she had done. "I don't need that bitch getting weak and start talking," Sadie said out loud, picking up her phone and dialing Tootsie's number.

Tootsie looked at her phone and saw that it was Sadie calling. She quickly hit the END button and sent her straight to voice mail. She wanted to concentrate on the coke-laced joint that she was placing to her lips. She felt guilty about what she had done.

Sadie had manipulated her into killing a man and the burden was weighing down on her soul. She took a deep pull of the blunt and smiled as the smoke tickled her lungs. It seemed to erase her pain.

Sadie had introduced her to the new high, and now, she couldn't get enough of it. She had been on a five-day binge, and the habit was causing her world to turn upside down.

Tootsie's grades at the university had been falling. She was missing classes, and her GPA which had been 3.5 dropped to a 1.5 quickly. She had received a letter from the dean's office stating that her academic scholarship had been voided because of her poor GPA. Once the semester was over, she would have to return to Alabama, the slums she called home. This stressed her out to the point where she was losing her hair.

Sadie had been acting standoffish to her lately, and she clung to the drugs to escape the pain even more. The thought kept revolving in her mind, *Sadie promised me that by killing Rock, we would become closer.* However, it seemed as if the opposite was happening. Sadie was pushing her farther and farther away. After the murder, Sadie gave her many excuses to stay away. She would only talk to her at certain times. Tootsie took another puff of the laced weed and felt the green monster—jealousy—brewing inside of her heart.

"I'm going to kill that bitch," Tootsie said, looking around her dorm room. Sadie had told her it would be better if they weren't around each other and that she should go back to school. At least until things blew over about the murder. But Tootsie saw straight through Sadie now.

Sadie made her move back to her dorm room. It was depressing for her to be there. She knew Sadie used her for what she wanted and now she was trying to get rid of her, slowly but surely.

Tootsie was so in love with Sadie and regardless of what Sadie made her do, Tootsie still wanted to be at her side. Without Sadie, her entire world was falling apart at a rapid pace.

Chapter Twelve

"Sis, I'm sorry to hear about Rock. I knew how much you cared for him," Carla said to Serenity over the phone.

"I can't believe he's gone," Serenity said sniffling.

"Do you want me to come get you so you can be here for the funeral?" Carla asked.

"No, I have a friend that will come with me. I'm good." Serenity wiped her nose, speaking lowly.

"Okay, if you need anything, just let me know, a'ight?"

"All right. I'll see you soon, sis. I love you," Serenity said, beginning to cry.

"I love you too, baby sis. I think I better come down there. You sure you don't want me to come get you?" Carla asked, her voice cracking.

"Thanks, but I think I can handle getting there. I don't know about keeping it together when I get there though."

"Don't worry, I'll be here for you. Call me anytime 'til then, okay?" Carla reinforced her support.

"See you soon, sis," Serenity said.

Carla hated to see or hear her baby sister cry. She wanted to hop on a plane when she found out but was stopped by her remembrance of their previous conversation about giving Serenity space to grow. Calling her seemed to be the better way of approaching her, rather than just showing up.

A week had passed, and Serenity cried, looking at Rock's corpse in the cherry oak casket. He didn't look like the man she had loved . Sadie's arm was around Serenity, comforting her.

Sadie was looking gloom on the outside, but on the inside, she was overjoyed. She flew to Chicago with Serenity for support, at least that's what she said. But in all truth, she was full of jealousy and wanted to keep a close tab on Serenity while she was away from college. Serenity was her prized trophy, and she was becoming more possessive of her by the day.

"It's okay, baby," Sadie said, handing her a handkerchief.

Serenity wore an all-black dress with very big, dark shades over her eyes to hide how much of an emotional wreck she was. She had just lost her first love, and she had no idea she was standing next to the person responsible for Rock's murder.

Sadie's eyes hid behind her tinted Cartier glasses, and she wore a black Coogi sweater with dark denims. Her acting as a support system for Serenity was working. The more she was there for her, the more it became evident that Serenity wouldn't leave her.

Serenity bent over, kissed Rock on his lips, and felt a chill race through her body. His face was now hard and cold, and tears rolled down her cheeks. "I will always love you, Rock," she whispered. Her teardrops fell on his face. Trembling, she stood up and walked back down the aisle with Sadie. She couldn't stay for the whole service. It was too much for her to handle. She wanted to stay there, but she just couldn't. She had too much guilt wrapped around her mind. Her body and mind were just too drained. The way he died made it much worse for her. She couldn't understand why someone would want to kill him.

Her heart weighed heavy when she thought about how they hadn't been on speaking terms. It was burdening her soul. *I wish I could have expressed how much I loved him one last time*, she thought, recalling his facial expression when she barely recognized him at the game. She could tell that he was hurt, because she was with Sadie. *If I wasn't high on that shit, I would have acted differently. But now I can never get a chance to make things right with him.*

Sadie protectively wrapped her arm around Serenity's waist and guided her toward the exit, rubbing her shoulders for comfort. The police report stated there were no suspects in the case and they had no idea who did the crime, which made Sadie a very happy woman.

Most likely, it would be put on the back burner with the homicide department.

Serenity's sister, Carla, paid her respects to Rock and dropped a flower in the casket, then headed out, following behind them.

Iris also paid her respects and vowed to throw a monkey wrench in Shawn P's hustling status just for Rock.

"Serenity," Carla said, stepping out of the church doors.

They were heading down the steps of the church. Serenity immediately recognized her sister's raspy, low voice and turned around. She and Sadie had just flown in, and she didn't have a chance to stop at home to see her sister. It was the first time she had seen her since she landed in the Windy City. It would be the first time they would speak face to face in months.

"Carla!" Serenity exclaimed, breaking away from Sadie and rushing into her arms.

Sadie instantly grew an attitude seeing Serenity run into another woman's arms. She intuitively knew Carla was gay by her short haircut and male attire. It was obvious to her that they were playing on the same team. She clenched her jaws tightly watching Carla embrace her woman.

Serenity never told Sadie about her older sister back home who was a lesbian. Sadie had no idea of their relationship, and her first reaction was jealousy and rage.

"Serenity!" Sadie barked, taking a step toward them.

"Oh, Sadie, I didn't tell you I had an older sister,"

Serenity said turning around. She thought about her sister's reaction seeing her with a lesbian. Immediately, Serenity grew uncomfortable. Her sister's face twisted when she looked at Sadie.

Carla looked her up and down. *Game recognize game*, she thought extending her hand, and they greeted each other just as gangsters do, with a shake and then a lock of the fist.

"Yo', I'm Carla," she said, but refrained from smiling.

"I'm Sadie," came the reply as Sadie sensed the tension and gave her a cold, hard stare.

Carla wanted to ask Serenity what was up with her, but decided to discuss that issue when they were alone. "Let's go home and get some food. Yeah, we need to talk," Carla said, wrapping her arm around Serenity.

Sadie didn't know exactly who Carla was in the game, but knew her brother was supplying her. There was something about her she didn't like. "Okay, let's go. My rental is around the corner." She didn't want Serenity out of her sight.

"Yeah, let's go. You can follow us," Carla stated, looking at Sadie.

"Serenity, you okay with that?" Sadie questioned her.

"Why wouldn't it be okay? She's my sister," Carla said, shooting Sadie a glare as she reached for Serenity. "Serenity, come on," Carla said firmly.

Carla and Serenity drove in silence. They had both been out of touch with each other. There was only one question on Carla's mind. *Why the fuck is Serenity with this bitch? That's the same stud I heard about.*

When they arrived at the house, Carla started to make something to eat without a word to her sister or Sadie. Serenity walked straight to her room to lie down until the food was ready.

Carla finished cooking and set the table. She called her sister down, but she wouldn't come out of her room. She just wanted to sleep. So Carla walked into the living room where Sadie was sitting and told her the food was ready. She walked back to the dining area, sat down, and began eating, not waiting for Sadie.

When Sadie got to the table, she smiled at Carla and sat down to eat.

"Umm . . . So, where you from?" Carla asked, trying not to sound upset. She was still unsure about the relationship Sadie had with her sister. She didn't want to jump on her without knowing the truth from Serenity.

Sadie looked in Carla's eyes, not backing down. "I'm from D.C. Maybe you heard of me, Sadie Smith," she said with a cold smile.

"Sadie Smith? That sounds familiar," Carla said, knowing exactly who she was, at least from what she had been told. But seeing Sadie up close, she knew she had seen her face before. "You know someone named Shawn P?" she asked with a closer look. She remembered seeing her face in a picture with Shawn P. It was framed and noticeable on the wall facing the front door at Shawn P's place. Every time she would go get her supply, she would see the picture. It was Sadie and Shawn P at the grand opening to one of the biggest strip clubs in D.C.

"Yeah, that's my brother. But how do you know him?" Sadie asked and pushed her plate to the side with a perplexed expression.

"I fuck with P. That's my man. We go back years, feel me?" Carla asked, hinting at her dealings with Shawn P. The tension in the room lessened, but she still wanted to know what was going on with her and Serenity. From her knowledge, her sister wasn't gay, and it was obvious that Sadie was.

She continued, "So what's your business with my baby sister?" she asked frankly, knowing all about how Sadie got down with her women. She turned girls out and used them.

"She's my friend. We're just close. I really don't think I should be revealing my relationship with your sister," Sadie cleared her throat and stood up. "I don't think that's any of your business," she said, releasing a small grin.

"I don't know what's going on with you two. But that girl in there . . ." Carla pointed to the back room where Serenity lay resting, "that's my flesh and blood, and I don't fuck around when it's comes to my family. If someone hurts her . . . I hurt them. Feel me?" she said with a man's swagger and a boss's tone.

Sadie chuckled and thought to herself, *I don't know who this bitch thinks she is, but I'ma let that slide THIS time.* "Okay, boss," Sadie said sarcastically, heading toward the front door with a smile. "Look, I'm about to go to my hotel room. Let baby girl . . . I mean, let Serenity know that I'll pick her up in the morning so we can head back home," Sadie said, hinting to Carla that this was more than a mere friendship.

Carla heard the front door close and shook her head in disgust as she stood up to clear the table. She wanted to go straight to Serenity's room and confront her, face-to-face, about everything she knew about this chick Sadie Smith.

Chapter Thirteen

The end of the semester was rapidly approaching, and Serenity's world was just getting back to normal. She never explained to her sister that once she left after Rock's funeral it was official that she was a lesbian. She often thought about Rock and realized he might not have been the only reason why she joined him at the same school. It was a place to find who she really was.

She looked over to Sadie who was sound asleep in her bed. Serenity sat at the vanity mirror that was in her bedroom and looked down at the small pile of coke on the desk. The sounds of the rainstorm from outside gave the room it's very own soundtrack.

Her reflection in the mirror caught her attention. She saw her bloodshot eyes and didn't recognize the face that stared backed at her. She had been up all night getting high off the blow and was quickly becoming something that she wasn't.

Serenity starting getting into drugs when she returned from Rock's funeral, feeling depressed. Sadie purposely left small piles of coke around to entice her. Now, she was hooked and couldn't get enough. Serenity used her pinky nail to line up the white substance. She swooped her head down and quickly snorted the lines, using her nose like a Dyson vacuum.

Her eyes began to water as she allowed the drug to take its course through her body. *What am I doing? What happened to me? This is not me. Look at me, look at me. Who are you?* The thoughts tumbled in her mind as she stared at the unknown face in the mirror. She had seen a drop in her grades, and her world was filled with sex, drugs, and partying all over again. At first, being with Sadie was exciting, but now, it was getting old. It definitely wasn't what she expected. The only thing she got from being with her was a bad coke addiction. She saw Sadie sit up and stretch her arms.

"What you doing over there, baby girl?" Sadie asked, wiping the sleep from her eyes.

"Hitting this candy you left out for me," Serenity said, using her pinky to line up another hit of coke.

"I want something to eat," Sadie said hungrily, focusing on Serenity's naked body.

"What do you want, a sandwich or something?" Serenity asked, standing up.

"No, not like that. I want . . . something . . . to . . . devour," Sadie said flicking her tongue, signaling that she wanted Serenity's pussy, nothing else.

Serenity smiled and walked over to the bed with her mind fully intoxicated by the drugs and the lust written all over her lover's face.

Sadie grabbed Serenity and pulled her down, landing on her back. She parted her legs and looked at her pink wound. She loved the way Serenity kept her juice box neatly groomed. She licked her thumb and placed it on Serenity's clitoris, rubbing it in a slow, circular motion.

Serenity closed her eyes and slowly started to grind. Her lips were getting wet from Sadie's tongue. She grabbed the sheets and began to moan. The moans first started in soft, low hums but eventually turned into loud, orgasmic yells as Sadie worked her thumb swiftly and expertly.

Finally, Sadie dove in between her legs and placed her tongue on Serenity's anus. She worked it slowly. Long ago, she had found out that Serenity loved to get her salad tossed. It became a part of Sadie's sexual repertoire when fucking Serenity.

"Damn, Sadie. Lick that ass," Serenity crooned, feeling an orgasm approaching.

Sadie stopped just in the nick of time, depriving Serenity of cumming, and went to her dresser and got her strap-on. She put it on and headed back to the bed, stroking her cock. She flipped Serenity into the doggie-style position.

Serenity wiggled her ass in anticipation and rubbed

her pussy, wanting Sadie to hurry up and enter her. She was at her peak and was high as ever. She loved the way coke made the sex feel. It took sex to another level and made it even more incredible. She didn't realize it, but she also had developed another addiction—sex. She was turning into Sadie's supersized freak, just the way Sadie wanted it.

Sadie guided the dark dildo into Serenity and began to pump rapidly. She went deep, shallow, fast, and eventually slow. She grabbed Serenity's ass, occasionally smacking it, making it jiggle from side to side, and slammed Serenity against her hard cock.

Serenity knew Sadie's strokes were better than Rock's. She knew it was fake, but it was better. She didn't have to worry about Sadie getting limp or busting off in a hurry. "Yeah, fuck me, Sadie . . . it feels sooo good, daddy . . ."

"Oh . . . oh, yeah, baby girl. Nut for daddy, baby," Sadie said, then licked her thumb and placed it in Serenity's other hole.

"Here I cum, daddy," Serenity moaned, pumping her ass back at Sadie. "I'm about to squirt," she yelled, feeling the greatest sensation ever approaching. In the midst of the bliss, she glanced back at Sadie. Unexpectedly, she saw a shadow at the window. Tootsie was watching them through the bedroom window. The rain poured down on her, making her shiver like she had been there for awhile. It startled Serenity, and she jumped up and screamed.

"What's wrong?" Sadie asked, confused by her actions.

"It's Tootsie," Serenity said, looking back at the window, but no one was standing there anymore. She sat up and held her chest, breathing hard.

"What do you mean? Are you sure?" Sadie asked, looking out the window, seeing nothing but rain hitting the glass. "Yo', how much coke did you snort?"

"I'm not crazy. I just saw that crazy, stalker bitch watching us have sex. I'm high, but not that damn high. I *know* what I saw," Serenity affirmed, covering up and keeping her eyes on the window.

Sadie stood up with the strap-on still attached and looked outside again and still saw nothing. She closed the curtains immediately and shook her head in disbelief. "That bitch is a problem," she whispered. She went over to comfort a noticeably shaken-up Serenity.

Chapter Fourteen

Tootsie kept seeing the images of Sadie sexing Serenity the same way Sadie used to sex her. But now, she was cut out of the picture and felt totally lost. She stared at the letter in her hand from the school explaining why she had to leave. They gave her until the end of the semester to pack her belongings and move out of the dorm. The semester would end in about three weeks. "Why fucking stay here for three more weeks?" she questioned herself, crying and packing her belongings into a suitcase.

She had been trying to call Sadie all day, but Sadie kept hanging up on her. After calling five times, she just got her voice mail. Finally, she received a text that read, LEAVE ME THE FUCK ALONE, YOU STUPID JUNKIE BITCH. DON'T EVER FUCKIN' CALL ME AGAIN. DON'T DO NOTHING, DUMB BITCH, 'CUZ THAT STUPID MOTHERFUCKA TAPED THAT SHIT.

Tootsie's heart crumbled. She finished packing her things and headed out of the dorm with two heavy suitcases and an oversized overnight bag. *I have to go to her until I can figure out what to do next,* she thought, walking down the hallway with her head hung low in shame. Students looked at her like she was nutty. Her world shattered ever since that awful night with Rock. She hoped once Sadie saw how desperate she was that she would make things right again.

Later on that night . . .

Sadie and Serenity were watching *American Gangster* while puffing on a blunt. Serenity was cuddled up in Sadie's arms on the sofa. The doorbell chimed through the house. Sadie looked toward the hallway and frowned when she looked at her watch and noticed it was just a little after midnight.

"Who the fuck is that coming over this late? I'm gonna kill these bitches if they think they coming up in here," Sadie said, lifting Serenity off her. "I'll be right back, baby girl," she said, walking toward the front door.

She looked through the side glass surrounding the door and saw Tootsie standing there with her suitcases on the porch. Sadie took a deep breath and shook her head in disbelief. She opened the door with an irritated expression.

"I'm glad you're home," Tootsie said, smiling and trying to step in, not even noticing Sadie's irritation.

"Hold up, ma! What do you think you're doing?" Sadie asked with malice in her voice.

"What do you mean?" Tootsie asked, still smiling. She looked into Sadie's eyes, clearly seeing her displeasure now. Suddenly, her smile disappeared and her face looked confused at Sadie's demeanor. "You never had a problem with me coming over before, and now that everything is dead and buried, what's the problem? But anyway, I got put out of the dorms. They said my scholarship was voided, so I need to stay here until I figure out what to do."

"Were you looking in my window the other night, Tootsie?" Sadie asked sternly.

Tootsie paused before she answered the question. She didn't think that Sadie saw her, but she knew Serenity did. *Did she see me? I guess not, if she's asking me if I was there.* "No, why would I do something like that?" she lied, picking up her luggage.

"Hold up. You can't stay here. I can pay for your bus ticket to go back home," Sadie said, preventing Tootsie from entering with her luggage. "You have to go," she stated loudly.

"What? What the hell you talking about, baby?" Tootsie asked in a begging manner, stepping closer to Sadie.

Sadie could smell the coke fumes reeking off Tootsie and by the look of her bucked eyes, she knew she was high on that shit. Sadie pushed Tootsie lightly, signaling her to back up.

"Uh-uh. You gots to get the fuck on, Tootsie. I told you I ain't fuckin' with you like that no more. Did you not get the hint when I cursed your ass out? Just fuckin' leave me the fuck alone or you will make me do something you gonna regret," Sadie warned her, losing her patience with her ex. She looked to see if Serenity was coming, then lowered her voice. Aggression laced her words. "Look, bitch, listen to me carefully. You and me are not like that no more. You better lay low and stay the fuck away from me," she said slowly and deliberately.

Tootsie's eyes began to water, and so many things ran through her head. *Sadie is rejecting me after all I did for her.*

"You and me are not like that, huh?" Tootsie said, repeating the words that scorched her brain, not wanting to believe them.

"That's right, you crazy, fuckin' bitch!" Sadie barked.

"I killed a man for you, daddy. Why are you doing me like this?" she whispered with her voice cracking.

"I don't know what the fuck you're talking about, ho. *You* did that!" Sadie snarled, lunging for Tootsie's neck.

Tootsie's small frame began to shake wildly as she struggled to get air. She tried to pry Sadie's fingers away, but Sadie's grasp was much too strong for her to fight back.

Sadie squeezed her neck hard and put her lips on Tootsie's ear. She whispered, "Listen, you fuckin' bitch, if I *ever* see your ass around here again, I will send the tape to the cops showing that *you* were the one who killed Rock. I can be very convincing. I just have to say you got jealous of my relationship with Serenity and killed Rock to hurt her. I don't ever want to see your stupid ass again. You hear me? *Ever!*" Sadie threatened, pushing Tootsie against the wall with all her might, causing a big thud to resonate throughout the house. From behind her, Sadie heard movement and knew that Serenity had gotten up.

"Is everything all right in there?" Serenity yelled out.

"Everything's good, baby girl. Go lie down again," Sadie replied quickly.

Tootsie continued to cry, knowing her world had just caved in. She had no one now that Sadie had pushed her out of her life. "That bitch here, huh? Is *that* why you wanted me to kill him? You just wanted her for yourself?" she said between sobs. "I hate you, Sadie Smith! I hate you," Tootsie yelled at the top of her lungs and grabbed her own hair. She yanked at it, trying to rip patches out from her own head. Then she started pounding her head against the wall like a madwoman. It was clear she was in the middle of a total psychological and emotional breakdown. She couldn't take the rejection anymore and ran past Sadie into the kitchen.

Sadie ran after her, not knowing her intentions. In the middle of the kitchen, she saw Tootsie with a long butcher knife in her hand.

"Get the fuck outta my house before I call the police, you crazy-ass bitch!" Sadie screamed, staring at her whacked-out eyes.

"Why . . . why don't you love me anymore, Sadie?" she whimpered.

Serenity had come into the kitchen at that point because of all the yelling and commotion.

Snot and tears streamed down Tootsie's face. She had lost all her dignity and no longer cared. She just wanted Sadie to love her and make things like they used to be. Little did she know, however, nothing would ever be the same again.

"Oh, shit! What the fuck is going on?" Serenity gasped, putting her hand over her mouth. She had walked in on what looked like a Stephen King horror movie. Tootsie looked deranged, waving the butcher knife around at Sadie.

"Put that damn knife down, Tootsie," Sadie ordered. She put both her hands in the air in surrender and inched toward her. "You're not thinking straight. You on that shit! You're as high as hell and acting fuckin' crazy, like a psycho. Now stop the fuckin' bullshit."

"Fuck you! I love you, but you don't see that. You're so far up this trick-ass bitch right here that you done turned fuckin' blind," Tootsie screamed, now pointing the knife at Serenity.

"Whoa, hold up," Serenity exclaimed, putting her hands up also and backing away.

"I did it for *you*!" Tootsie roared at Sadie.

Sadie grew nervous hearing those words come out of her mouth. She knew Tootsie was talking too much. She needed to do something before she revealed her dirty secret to Serenity.

"Look, Tootsie, calm down. I do love you, okay," Sadie said, totally changing her tone and demeanor. She put on a fake smile, trying to calm Tootsie down and get her to release the knife.

"No, you don't. You're just saying that. You think I'm fuckin' stupid, don't you?" Tootsie shouted with hatred filling her heart.

"I do love you, baby. Just put down the knife and let's talk about it, okay?" Sadie said, stepping closer to her.

Tootsie looked at Serenity and rage totally possessed her body and mind. She thought about stabbing the knife directly into Sadie's heart, but instead, she lowered the knife to her own wrist and sliced with vengeance.

"Tootsie!" Sadie screamed, trying to grab the knife away and stop her from hurting herself. She grabbed the knife and threw it away, and Tootsie collapsed in her arms. "Call 911!" she ordered Serenity. "Why did you have to do that, Tootsie? Why?" she said, cradling Tootsie, rocking her back and forth as Tootsie cried like a baby.

Blood flowed from Tootsie's wrist like a faucet.

Chapter Fifteen

Sadie sat in the back of the ambulance with Tootsie and watched the paramedics wrap her wrist up tightly. She knew that she would have to put on a front to keep Tootsie happy and quiet for the time being. She told Serenity to stay at her house while she made sure Tootsie was safely admitted to the hospital. But the real reason she wanted Serenity to stay there was because of the fear that Tootsie would expose her.

"Everything is going to be okay, Tootsie. Baby, I'm sorry, I must be buggin'," Sadie said, gently stroking her hair. The ambulance bumped and swayed its way along to the hospital, its siren blaring. "I'm sorry, baby," Sadie said, kissing her forehead.

"You promise everything will be okay?" Tootsie whimpered in a whisper.

"I promise, baby. I love you," Sadie lied once again.

"I love you, too, daddy," Tootsie stated with a soothed soul.

Sadie walked out of the hospital and saw Serenity parked by the pickup lane waiting for her. She had called her to come get her four hours after admitting Tootsie. She convinced Tootsie to be admitted to the mental ward just until things blew over. She promised her that by the time she finished the medical evaluation, Serenity would be out of the picture. Then they would start their life together again. She smiled, knowing that she had just sold Tootsie a dream. The semester would be over soon, and she planned to be long gone by the time Tootsie got out. Sadie just told her whatever she wanted to hear to make her happy at the moment. She planned on convincing Serenity to enroll in another school with her and leave town for good.

"Hey, baby," Sadie said tiredly, getting into the car. She leaned over and kissed Serenity before she pulled off.

"Is everything okay? That bitch done lost all of her marbles. Damn!" Serenity said, maneuvering the luxury vehicle away from the curb.

"Yeah, she got a serious mental problem. That's what those drugs do to you. I know you've . . . both of us . . . have been hitting that candy, but she took it to a whole 'nother level by smoking that shit," Sadie said, leaving out the fact that she was the one that got her hooked.

"I don't feel safe. You gotta do something. Change

them locks and put fuckin' cameras up or I can't stay there," Serenity demanded.

"All right, if that's what's gonna make you safe, then fine. Consider it done. But you know, I was thinking maybe moving wouldn't be a bad idea. I think you know what I'm saying. This place is becoming old and bad news. It'll be just me and you. No old faces, no wild sex parties, just me and you," Sadie smiled and placed her hand on Serenity's thigh.

"You sure you're willing to give all that up? All those women?" Serenity asked.

"Well, if you want more pussy in the mix, then it's fine with me. I got all I need right here," Sadie responded.

"I love you, Sadie Smith," Serenity said smiling.

Sadie had a way of making a woman feel like she was the queen. She had Serenity wrapped around her finger.

"I love you too, baby girl. Now, let's go home and get some rest. We got class in the morning, and it's going to be a busy week lookin' for a new place," Sadie said, laying her head on the headrest and turning up the Sade CD.

Chapter Sixteen

Tootsie sat in the small room and talked to herself. She tried to stop herself from thinking about killing Serenity.

Sadie promised her that she would be right by her side through the evaluation process on the mental ward, but she disappeared after Tootsie was admitted. She looked down at the bandages that were wrapped around her wrist. She thought about that horrible night and decided Serenity was the reason that she was there.

The only reason Tootsie remained in the hospital was to make Sadie happy. She could have checked herself out at any given time after a couple of days of observation, but she chose not to. When she realized Sadie was probably never going to show up, she became hateful. She lost her mind and the only thing she wanted at that point was revenge. Revenge on Serenity for taking the only person that she had in her life—Sadie Smith.

Tootsie walked out of the room and to the front desk. She asked the nurse for her release forms. She was on her way to show Serenity what the consequences were for ruining her life with Sadie. *That bitch is gonna pay*, she thought, signing the final release form.

"These bitches must think I'm certified psychotic . . ." Tootsie whispered under her breath while sitting at the edge of her hospital bed, waiting for her nurse to return with her release forms. "Oh, I'm gonna show them, all right."

"Okay, sweetie, I just need you to sign these papers, and you must see one of the listed psychiatrists on this sheet, okay?" the nurse smiled and handed her the pen.

"No problem." Tootsie signed the release forms with a bright smile.

"Aren't you happy. Well, I would be too, if I were you," the nurse said, handing Tootsie her copies of all the signed discharge papers.

Tootsie got into the elevator smiling as she left the ward. As soon as she got outside, she reached into her bag for her phone.

Serenity and Sadie were getting ready to go out for dinner and maybe go to the strip club afterward. Serenity was applying her makeup in the bathroom and was all smiles at the thought of being at Sadie's side. She was wearing one of the many Prada dresses Sadie bought her on their weekly shopping sprees together.

"Baby girl, can you come in here a minute, please." Sadie neatly placed a signature blue Tiffany's box on the dresser and stood in front of it, blocking its view from the entrance of the bedroom.

"What's up? I'm almost ready. I just have to put on my jewelry," Serenity said, walking into the bedroom.

"Well, that's what I wanted to talk to you about." Sadie stepped to the side so the Tiffany box was in full view. "I noticed you didn't have any bracelets."

Serenity's eyes focused on the blue box as she walked closer to Sadie. "Is that for me?"

"Baby girl, what a silly question. Just open it," Sadie replied.

Serenity slowly untied the white ribbon and uncovered the box. It was a beautiful diamond tennis bracelet shaped with Xs and Os. It was gorgeous. "Oh, Sadie, this is just beautiful," Serenity happily exclaimed, hugging Sadie and kissing her passionately.

"You sure you want to go out? With a kiss like that, I might just want to stay home under the sheets," Sadie said with a mischievous grin.

"Yeah, I bet you would . . . we plenty of time for all that. Come on, I'm starving. Beside, my mouth is watering for lobster," Serenity laughed.

Tootsie waited outside Sadie's crib in a black Honda Accord Coupe. After leaving the hospital, she made a few phone calls and got a rental for several weeks. She knew exactly where Sadie stashed her cash and drugs since she had stayed with her for so long. Tootsie still had a key to the house. "That stupid bitch probably ain't even changed the lock," she muttered under her breath.

"Come on, let's go. You locked the door?" Serenity asked, stepping outside toward the car.

"Yeah, go ahead." They walked to the car, and Sadie opened the passenger door for Serenity. As she walked around the car, she paused for a second and looked at a black Honda parked across the street. She couldn't see anyone inside. Then she walked around to the driver's side and climbed in.

"Baby, everything okay?" Serenity asked, looking at Sadie.

"Yeah . . . umm . . . yeah . . ." Sadie said, feeling that something wasn't quite right, but she shook it off. "Yeah, it's all good, baby girl. Let's go have some fun."

They backed out of the driveway and drove in the opposite direction of the black Honda.

Tootsie saw them come out of the house and slouched down in her car seat. After hearing the car pull out of the driveway, she eased herself up, then sat and waited for at least twenty minutes to make sure they wouldn't return just in case they forgot something.

Satisfied the coast was clear, she reached for a small duffel bag on the passenger seat, then walked to the door. She pulled out her key and inserted it into the keyhole, praying that it would work. "Please open . . . please open . . ." She turned the key slowly and heard the click of the lock unlatching. "I *knew* that bitch was stupid. She's so fuckin' pussy whipped by that bitch Serenity she forgot I was here before Serenity got my sloppy seconds," Tootsie smirked, entering the house.

She entered and closed the door behind her quickly so as not to attract any neighbors' unwanted attention. Inhaling deeply, she went straight to the bedroom and turned the dimmer switch on the light down on low. She glanced at the neatly made bed and walked straight over to Sadie's closet. She pulled out one of Sadie's expensive button-up shirts.

Stripping naked, Tootsie slipped on the shirt. She smelled Sadie's scent and desperately wanted to be next to her, to touch her. Glancing over at the bed, she climbed in it. She stuffed one of the pillows between her legs and snuggled against the other pillow on Sadie's side of the bed with thoughts of all of the erotic sex they had shared floating through her head.

Soon, her eyes caught a glimpse of a dainty blue box on the dresser. Tootsie's heart began to race. She jumped out of the bed and rushed over to the dresser, picked up the blue box, and threw it across the room in a blind rage. Suddenly, every item on top the dresser flew off and ricocheted against the wall.

Tootsie stormed into the kitchen pantry and searched for an old, scratched-up cookie jar. She knew that Sadie kept her stash of cocaine there for all her sex parties.

She found it and opened the lid.

"Oh, hell, yeah. I could get at least ten Gs for this and

still have some candy for myself. Fuckin' stupid-ass bitch. Now I'ma go take all your fuckin' cash and leave you a little pleasant surprise," Tootsie laughed insanely.

She quickly moved around the house, remembering all Sadie's little money coves and emptying each one of them. Then she walked over to her duffel bag and unzipped it. Tootsie's nose turned at the scent. *Definitely* not Chanel. She pulled out a pair of latex gloves, put them on, and then grabbed a few tied bags filled with fresh dog shit. Tootsie was on a mission. She emptied the first bag on Sadie's beige, Italian leather designer sofa, using the now-empty bag to smear the dog shit everywhere. Then she decided to spread the other bags of shit on Sadie's notorious throne, a few white walls, the dining table, and the bed Sadie and Serenity slept in.

Tootsie enjoyed destroying Sadie's material possessions. With this much shit splashed around the house, Sadie was going to be putting out a lot money for new stuff. With all of her secret money stashes raided, it was going to be at least a few days before she could get a hold of some serious cash.

"This should throw a monkey wrench in any plans they got going on. Stupid bitches." Tootsie laughed coldheartedly, painting a huge brown smiley face on the wall facing the entrance with a little message.

Sadie opened the door to her home, allowing Serenity in first. Suddenly, Serenity stopped dead in her tracks. She quickly reached for the lights in disbelief. The wall in front of them displayed a nasty message with a smiley face.

U BEEN SHIT ON! CAN U SMELL ME?

"That motherfuckin' bitch," Sadie screamed in rage. "Come on, let's go!" she yelled at Serenity, causing her to jump.

"Where are we going? You don't have to yell either." Serenity walked out the door immediately with an attitude.

"Look, I'm sorry, baby girl . . . it's just that this fuckin' bitch done fucked up my house, and all I want to do is find her and wrap a rope around her neck 'til she expires." Pissed-off did not describe how Sadie felt. "Come on, let's go to the Marriott. This bitch done blew my whole fuckin' vibes. Damn."

"What are we gonna do about the house?" Serenity asked, concerned.

"Get a new one. I hope you didn't have anything too special in there," Sadie replied grimly.

"Well, you really don't know who did it or how bad it really is in there. What about your money and shit? You don't care about that shit?"

"Don't worry, Serenity, I'll take care of everything. Whatever you got in there that can be salvaged, it will be. Now let's just forget about it. I'm tired. We gotta get to the hotel. Tomorrow is gonna be a long-ass day for us."

"All right, baby, let's go," Serenity said.

Chapter Seventeen

The semester was coming to the end, and Serenity had just completed her finals and was waiting for Sadie in the courtyard of the campus. She looked at her cell phone to check the time and wondered where Sadie could be. *She's always on time.* She was now ten minutes late. She saw Raya walk directly past her. Then she realized she hadn't seen her ex-roommate in a long time. Lately, all her time had been consumed with classes and Sadie.

"Hey, Raya," Serenity called out.

Raya turned around and walked over to her. "Hey, Serenity," Raya replied, smiling. She threw her arms around her and squeezed tightly. "I haven't seen you in a while. How are you?"

"I'm good. How have you been?"

"I'm okay. You're big stuff around campus now. I heard you and Sadie are official and everyone else has gotten kicked to the curb. Damn, I didn't know you could put it on her like that. I mean, I know you got some good pussy, but damn, girl, you done hit the jackpot," Raya teased playfully.

"Girl, chill out," Serenity said, embarrassed.

"Oh, yeah, your sister called the room the other day. She said she couldn't get in contact with you. You didn't tell her you switched your dorm room?" Raya asked.

"Yeah, I guess I forgot. Okay, I'll give her a call. I just been so busy with school and all. Don't have much time for anything it seems like," Serenity said, realizing she hadn't spoken with her sister in quite a while.

"Yeah, right. If that's what you say," Raya said just before she burst out laughing.

Serenity laughed along with her and didn't notice Sadie approaching.

Sadie threw her arm around Serenity, startling her, and glared at Raya as if she were her worst enemy.

"Let's go," Sadie said, irritated.

"Okay, but let me introduce you to my—"

"Let's go, I said," Sadie cut her off, talking between clenched teeth. She yanked her arm and walked toward the parking lot where she parked.

Raya looked confused, wondering what the hell that was all about.

"Nobody ain't trying to holla at your chick. Damn," Raya said loudly with her full attitude. She walked to her next class, shaking her head in disbelief.

"What's up with that? Damn, Raya is just a friend. She

was my roommate," Serenity tried to explain to Sadie seeing how upset she was.

Sadie remained quiet but clenched her jaws tightly, flexing the muscles in her strong jawbone. They both got into the car. Serenity tried to get Sadie to talk, but she only got the silent treatment.

"Sadie, talk to me," Serenity yelled, slamming her hands on the dashboard.

Without warning, Sadie thrust her hand out and punched Serenity in the eye. Her jealousy got the best of her.

"You shouldn't have been in that bitch's face. You my bitch . . . You don't talk to that ho-ass bitch," Sadie said with malice, her brows beginning to sweat. She was enraged and at the boiling point.

Serenity held her eye and tried to regain her vision that was temporarily disoriented.

Sadie gripped the steering wheel tightly and shot her a cold glance.

Serenity couldn't believe that Sadie had just punched her. "Why did you hit me?" she screamed, reaching over and digging her nails into Sadie's face.

Sadie swerved in traffic, trying to stop Serenity from ripping skin off her face.

"Get yo motherfuckin' hands off me, bitch. What the fuck is your problem?" Sadie screamed back, gripping Serenity's neck and forcing her head against the passenger-side window.

Sadie pulled into her driveway and gave Serenity a

hard slap across the face. Then she jumped out of the car and rushed over to the passenger side and pulled Serenity by her hair from the car and dragged her to the porch. The more Sadie thought about Serenity conversing with Raya, the angrier she got. She slapped her again, then she opened the front door and threw Serenity inside.

Serenity kicked and screamed, losing her balance and falling to the floor. She tried to get away from Sadie, but Sadie just kept slapping her. "Stop fuckin' hitting me, bitch. I'ma fuckin' call the cops. Stop . . . Stop . . ." Serenity pleaded with her.

Sadie completely lost it. "You *mine!* You hear me?" Sadie yelled, then stormed out the front door, slamming the door behind her.

Serenity cried. Her face ached from the brutal slaps inflicted by the woman who supposedly loved her. She lay in the middle of the floor, sobbing in pain. Her mind instantly went to Rock, and she remembered he promised he would never hit her. She missed him more than ever now. She lay there sobbing.

Chapter Eighteen

Serenity looked into the mirror and examined the bruises on her face from Sadie's attack and began to cry again. "How did I get myself into this?" she wailed out loud. She couldn't see her true self anymore. All she saw was a battered, lost woman. She had become a totally different person and was at the end of her rope.

"Fuck this shit!" she yelled. Storming into the bedroom, she grabbed her empty luggage bags from the closet and threw them on the bed. She opened them and starting throwing her clothes in. "I'm leaving this crazy bitch! I can't take this shit no more," she said grabbing her clothes off the rack in the closet. She went back and forth from the closet to the bed until she had removed all of her clothes from the closet.

When she went back to make sure she had all of her things, she saw a Gucci bag on the top shelf that Rock had bought her. She figured Sadie threw it up there. She pulled the stepladder out and snatched the bag from the shelf. She almost stumbled to the floor. The bag was heavier than she expected. She opened the bag and found a camcorder inside.

"What the fuck is this?" Serenity said, pulling it out of the bag. It looked familiar, and she remembered that Rock used to have one just like it. "Since this was in my bag, I'm taking this shit, too!" she defiantly said.

With her curiosity kicking in, Serenity wanted to see exactly what freaky shit Sadie had on tape. She also wanted to make sure it was not she that was on the tape. She opened it up, hoping the battery wasn't dead. Then she pressed POWER and on it came. She got excited and pulled out the screen, then pushed PLAY. Showtime!

What she saw made her heart damn near stop beating. She held the camcorder in front of her and watched the scene unfold. It was Rock getting oral sex from Tootsie in a hotel room. Serenity dropped the camera and placed her hand over her mouth in complete shock. She gathered herself together the best she could after seeing Rock on the screen. With trembling hands, she picked up the camcorder again and sat on the floor to watch, mesmerized.

Tootsie was sucking on his dick, and he was so into it. He didn't see her reach below the bed and pull out the 9 mm pistol. Nor did he see her raise the gun and shoot him point-blank, square between the eyes.

The sound of the gunshot made Serenity jump. It felt

so real, like she was there in the room when it happened. Serenity couldn't move. She just sat there frozen and stared at the camera screen in horror. There was her first love lying dead on the bed. Finally she knew how he died. *Why does Sadie have this camcorder?* As Serenity sat there, mulling over the murder, the next thing she saw stunned her even more.

As Tootsie stood up with the smoking gun in her hand, trembling, the sound of a door opening and closing could be heard. Next, Sadie appeared on the screen, taking the gun from Tootsie and kissing her on the forehead. Serenity heard her say, "You did a good job, baby girl." Then Sadie scanned the room and wiped everything down. After glancing in the direction of the TV, she walked up to the camera and look closely at it.

"This nigga was recording this shit," Serenity heard through the speakers. She watched Sadie pick up the camera and show her face clearly in the frame just before flicking the power switch off, leaving the screen blue.

Serenity buckled over and vomited.

"What the fuck . . ." a voice said, startling Serenity.

She quickly looked back and saw Sadie standing in the doorway. Moving her arms slowly, she put the camcorder behind her back. "Oh, I don't feel so good, baby. Can you get some paper towels to clean this mess up?" she asked with a shaking voice and a racing heart.

"What the fuck is this? You going somewhere? Did I tell you to pack your shit?" Sadie blurted out. She walked over to the bed and flipped open the luggage.

She then approached Serenity and towered over her. "What's behind your back?"

"Nothing," Serenity lied, scooting backward.

Sadie swiftly reached down and grabbed the camcorder from her grasp. "Oh, so I see you found out my little secret," she smiled coldly and gripped the back of Serenity's neck with her free hand. "Look, baby, I did this for us. He was getting in the way of what we have. He couldn't give you what I could. It's better this way," she said, tightening her grip on Serenity.

Serenity pretended to be calm, unafraid of Sadie. But she couldn't hold the tears from falling after witnessing Rock getting murdered. She couldn't keep her composure. She sobbed uncontrollably. The only image she could see was the look in Rock's eyes when he opened them and saw Tootsie pointing the gun at him. The camera caught the split second of fear expressed on his face before he was blown away.

She nodded to Sadie in agreement, but it was obvious that she was afraid. She was terrified and knew she had to get out of the house before something else happened. She was going to go straight to the police and get this bitch locked up for good. Then she was going to call her sister.

"You're hurting me, Sadie," Serenity said, pulling away from her, but the grip only got stronger. Now she was in pain. "Fuckin' let go of me!" Serenity screamed, trying move away.

Sadie became enraged and punched Serenity dead in the nose, causing blood to spew.

"Aghhh!" Serenity screamed, trying to stand up and run.

"I knew that you weren't going to understand that I did it for us. Don't you love me?" Sadie mumbled with watery eyes. Quickly, she dropped to one knee and began to stroke Serenity's hair and tried to comfort her as a mother would her child. In the next moment, she flipped out, thinking that Serenity would never love her like she loved Rock. She became infuriated, grabbed Serenity's face, and struck her again with all of her might. Sadie had lost her mind.

Serenity was seeing stars. She placed both of her hands on the floor, trying to hold steady. Bile began to rise in her throat once more.

Sadie calmed down once again. But she knew if she didn't do something drastic, this would come back to bite her in the ass. She knew Serenity would be loyal to Rock and go to the police with the truth. She stood up and began to pace the room with a worried look. She had mixed emotions and became overwhelmed.

Coldly, she looked down at Serenity, who was crying while holding her bloody face. Sadie had made up her mind. She knew what she had to do. She picked up the heavy brass lamp on the nightstand and struck Serenity in the back of her head, knocking her out cold. Then she calmly placed the lamp back on the nightstand and reached for her blunt left in the ashtray. She smoked and started putting her plan together. She was about to end all the chaos once and for all.

Serenity lay there as still as death.

Chapter Nineteen

Sadie circled around the chair, her Tims hitting the hardwood floor of the deserted auditorium and echoing throughout.

Serenity sat bound in the chair, still knocked out cold and bleeding from the nose and mouth.

Sadie had dragged her to the film room of the empty movie production hall. Since it was the weekend, she knew there would be no interruptions for what she was about to do. She just finished setting up the camera to focus squarely on Serenity. Serenity was about to become a movie star. Sadie was going to broadcast Serenity's death to the entire campus after she admits to killing her ex-boyfriend Rock. "Wake up, bitch! It's showtime!" she yelled, smacking Serenity across the face.

Serenity was groggy. She came to but didn't know where she was. Her vision was blurred, and her head ached furiously from the blow from the lamp earlier.

"Where am I?" Serenity managed to say utter, trying to make sense of the situation. The last thing she remembered was being in Sadie's room. She tried to move her limbs but realized that she had been tied up. Her movement was limited.

Sadie pulled out her gun and began to trace Serenity's lips with the barrel. "We could have had something special, but you had to go and fuck it up," she said with anger building in each word. "And now, you're about to suffer the consequences of your actions. I'm fuckin' Sadie Smith, the only bitch that can get away with this," she said arrogantly, striking Serenity in the face with the butt of her gun. "Now, hit this, bitch," she said and forced Serenity to snort the coke she put in front of her.

Serenity let out a loud grunt. Her right eye began to swell shut. The coke enhanced everything she felt. "Sadie, why are you doing this? I won't say anything about Rock. Just untie me so we can talk this out," Serenity pleaded, swaying back and forth in agony.

"Do you really think I believe you?" Sadie asked, starting to pace around the room. She walked to the stand that the camera was sitting on and grabbed a syringe that was filled with uncut heroin. She had gotten it from her brother. "I have a deal for you," she said, picking up the needle. "I'm going to give you this needle, and I want you to read from this card that I'm going to hold up. If you do that, I'll let you live. If not . . . I'ma shoot you right in the fuckin' head." She hit Serenity again with the butt of the gun.

"What?" Serenity asked in confusion, seeing double from the blow she had just taken.

"You heard me, bitch. You have two choices: read this card and look in the camera while you do it or fuckin' die," Sadie yelled and punched Serenity in the gut with all of her might. She set the syringe on the stand that was next to Serenity and then began to untie her hands. It was showtime. She positioned herself behind the camera and pushed the record button. Then she held up the cue cards with the large writing displaying exactly what Sadie wanted her to say.

Of course, Sadie had no intention of letting Serenity live, but she was not going to tell her that. She merely wanted to exonerate herself from the death of Rock before she killed Serenity and made it look like a suicide. She had rigged it so that her broadcast would be seen on the JumboTron that sat in the middle of the campus. She had it all planned out, and it was just moments before Serenity would be dead. Sadie could then move on.

What the fuck is going on? This bitch is crazy. Oh my God, try to stay calm . . . stay calm. I have to find a way out of this, Serenity thought, looking into the camera and then at Sadie who was standing behind it pointing the gun at her.

"Read it, bitch," Sadie whispered ominously in a very low voice. She held the cue card in one hand and placed her finger on the trigger of the gun in her other hand.

"I have been through so much this last year, and I'm at the end of my rope. I saw the love of my life die . . .

because of me! I killed Rock!" Serenity said, beginning to cry even harder. She tried to regain her composure. She gripped the chair tightly and began to hyperventilate. She couldn't believe what was coming out of her mouth.

"Put the needle to your arm, now!" Sadie whispered with bloodshot eyes and full of hate.

Serenity looked at the syringe full of the deadly cocktail. Snot and tears continued to flow. She shook her head, trying to convince herself not to go through with it. With shaking hands, she put the syringe to her arm and stared into the camera. She began to wonder how she got herself into this position. As she held the needle to her arm, she glanced at the camera one last time and whispered, "I don't want to live anymore."

Sadie turned off the camera and pointed her gun at Serenity's head.

"Sadie, you don't have to do this. I love you so much, baby. Don't do it," Serenity begged, trying to do anything to stop Sadie.

"Shut up! Shut up! You don't love me, bitch. You love that fuckin' dead nigga! That's who you love. So now I'ma reunite yo ass with him, and y'all can fuck each other for eternity in the afterlife. You wasn't fuckin' bicurious or gay. Yo ass just wanted your pussy ate. I should have never fucked with you. You fucked my head all up. I really loved you!" Sadie yelled with tears in her eyes.

Sadie knew that she couldn't shoot Serenity because it wouldn't look like a suicide. And it was only a matter of time before people came looking for Serenity or came into the auditorium. She had to move quickly. "You better put that needle in your arm, or I will shoot your ass. At least with the needle, it will be painless, almost like you're going to sleep," she said in a twisted way, trying to convince Serenity to pick the lesser of the two deaths.

Serenity's eyes began to roll to the back of her head. The drama was too much for her soul to bear, and she went into shock.

"What the fuck?" Sadie asked as she inched closer to Serenity and saw the whites in her eyes. She got closer and attempted to grab the needle. It didn't matter who injected the poison as long as it got into her arm.

Before Sadie's hand touched the needle, however, Serenity opened her eyes wide and plunged the needle in Sadie's neck, injecting all of it. She had been faking the whole time, and it worked like a charm. She watched Sadie drop her gun and begin to convulse. She saw how "painless" the death would have been, realizing Sadie was lying all along. It was actually one of the most excruciating ways to die, and Sadie just got a dose of her own medicine.

"Die, you fuckin' crazy-ass bitch," Serenity said, crying.

Sadie fell on the floor and began to squirm and writhe as bloody foam bubbled out of her mouth and nose.

Serenity coldly watched because Sadie had wanted to do the same thing to her.

After a moment, Sadie's breath became shallower. She clutched her neck and struggled for air. Her eyes began to roll to the back of her head.

Serenity watched her and cried. She was an emotional wreck.

Finally Sadie stopped moving and her eyes became vacant. She was dead.

"I hate you! I hate you!" Serenity screamed, untying her legs from the chair and standing up. But she instantly tumbled down, feeling dizzy. She pulled herself up onto the chair and began to yell for help. By a miracle she was alive, and for that, she was grateful. The drama was finally over.

Unable to walk, Serenity crawled down the long hallway, yelling for help. Her vision was blurry and doubled. She felt that she was about to pass out. Her head was spinning, and tears blinded what little vision she had, thinking about what she had just done. Just as she reached the double doors of the entrance of the film hall, she fainted in front of a group of students, beaten and battered.

"Someone get some help. Call 911, quickly," one student shouted to the crowd, cradling Serenity.

Epilogue

Serenity lay on the stretcher as EMS prepared to take her to the hospital for treatment. Another man walked alongside the stretcher, trying to get answers out of her. He was a tall, slender man wearing a trench coat; typical detective wear. He had sent a uniformed officer immediately over to Sadie's house to retrieve the video of Rock's death. Serenity was injured and had a concussion, but she was going to be okay for the most part.

"I'll be at the hospital to finish questioning you. If everything you told me checks out, you should be home resting tonight," the detective said, putting away his notepad and pen.

Serenity had told him everything that happened. She told him the videotape would show Sadie and Tootsie were responsible for Rock's death.

Sadie also was on a stretcher, but she was on her way to the morgue's freezer. A white sheet lay over her head, and her arm hung off the edge of the stretcher under the the sheet.

A huge crowd formed and became spectators to the grisly affair. All of a sudden, a Benz pulled up, almost hitting the crowd of students. Shawn P jumped out with his shirt off. He had gotten a call moments earlier informing him about his sister's demise. He rushed over to the campus, not believing that his sister would take it this far. He tried to get to his sister, but the police who were controlling the crowd, stopped him. "No!" he yelled recognizing the tattoos on Sadie's hand. "No! What the fuck happened to my sister?" he yelled, breaking down in a cop's arms. His only sibling was gone. All of the attention was on Shawn P screaming at the top of his lungs, crying for his sister.

Nobody saw a distraught Tootsie walking up with a chrome .45 at her side. She stood at the side of the back entrance of the ambulance with tears streaming down her face.

The detective at Serenity's side was headed over in Shawn P's direction to get some more questions answered.

Tootsie's hand shook when raising the gun. She pointed it at Serenity, who was about to be put into the ambulance by EMS. They were so busy watching the commotion they paused and didn't see anyone lurking at the side of the ambulance.

Serenity noticed Tootsie. It seemed as if everything

went down in slow motion to her. She saw the hateful, wild stare in Tootsie's eyes when she pointed the gun at her head. Before she could say or do anything, Tootsie let off two shots—one catching Serenity in the chest, and the other hitting Serenity in the head, killing her on contact.

The EMS dropped the stretcher and took cover. The entire crowd scattered in different directions, causing complete pandemonium. The officers instantly reached for their guns, but before they could even aim at Tootsie, she turned the gun and placed it in her mouth and sent a slug ripping through her cranium, dropping her to the ground.

Serenity woke up with a terrified look on her face. She slowly opened her eyes and looked around the room to see Carla sleeping in a chair beside her. She tried to speak but gagged on a tube sticking out of her mouth. She snatched the tube away and a beeping started to sound loudly.

Carla woke up to see Serenity removing the IV needle in her arm. "Serenity, what in the world . . . sis . . . leave that alone. You're okay now. You're at the hospital. Please, Serenity, stop." Carla reached for her and hugged her and tears formed.

"What happened? I had this crazy dream that Sadie was trying to kill me and Tootsie did kill me. How did I get here? What happened?" Serenity asked, crying like a newborn baby.

"Don't worry about what happened. The main thing

now is that you're safe," Carla said, fighting her own tears back.

"What's going on in here?" a nurse demanded, charging in.

"Ahh, she woke up, and I guess couldn't breathe, so she pulled that tube out," Carla stated.

"Well, I'm happy to see she's awake. When she came into the emergency room, her initial exam revealed some broken ribs and internal bleeding. Then her body went into shock, and she couldn't breathe on her own, so they hooked her up to an assisted breathing machine and sent her off to surgery," the nurse explained while inserting a new IV needle into Serenity's arm and removing the rest of the tubing taped to the side of her face.

"Nurse, why can't I remember anything?" Serenity asked, puzzled.

"Well, I'm no doctor, but I think the skull fracture on your head explains a lot. Don't worry, it will all come back to you. It's not lost forever. Honestly, I wouldn't want to remember a thing if I were you," the nurse replied with a terse smile. "Now, take it easy. Don't try to get up without any help. Just push that nurse icon on the side of your bed, and someone will come in to help you. My name is Ms. Salt."

"Thank you, Ms. Salt. My sister will help me while she's here," Serenity said, becoming more at ease.

"Sis, I'm . . . so sorry I wasn't there any sooner . . . I just—"

"Carla, stop, please. This is my entire fault I got involved with someone and something I knew nothing about. My curiosity led me to this whole disastrous outcome. You have nothing to apologize for. If anything, I should be the one saying how sorry I am. Sorry that I pushed you away, and sorry because I should have come to you when things got crazy," Serenity said in a low voice.

"Listen, you know me. I'm not one to tell you I told you so, but . . ."

"Oh, Carla, stop the bullshit." Serenity reached for her sister and hugged her tightly.

"So are you going to tell me what happened or not?" Serenity asked with a little smile on her face.

"All you need to know is that bitch Sadie is at the morgue on ice and Tootsie is locked away in some mental institution awaiting trial. She ain't coming out for a while," Carla said, laughing.

"Did the police get the tape?" Serenity asked.

"Yes, the detective said that was the only thing you were saying in and out of consciousness. I can't believe half the shit that bitch was doing to you. Damn, I only wish I could have been more—"

"Ahh, stop. There ain't nothing you could have done. That bitch was fine as hell even though she was crazy," Serenity chuckled. "Come on, let's watch some TV. Ms. Salt was right. I really don't want to remember that dreadful day anyway," she said to lighten the mood.

"You know you going to have to see somebody, right? You know your head ain't right." Carla laughed but looked at Serenity with the utmost seriousness.

As they flipped through the channels, they came across breaking news. Carla turned up the volume.

"Vivian 'Tootsie' Richards is awaiting trial at the Psychiatric Institute-Richmond. The DA has filed murder charges against her for the murder of Rock Stevenson, one of the top college football athletes scouted this year for the NFL Draft. He was discovered dead in a hotel room in the downtown D.C. area. Ms. Richards's well-known defense attorney has brought two motions for dismissal due to mental anguish and suffering and a technicality when she was arrested. When we requested a comment by the DA, he declined. The trial is set to start in two weeks."

Serenity and Carla stared at each other not wanting to believe that it was even possible for her to be set free.